DANCING WITH GUILT

BARRE TO BAR
BOOK FOUR

SUMMER COOPER

LOVY BOOKS

Roxie

oo many secrets. Too many lies. It was all falling apart, everything she touched just shattered in her hands like broken glass, to disappear into the void. She wanted to scream but something had stolen her voice. No sound came out, only a hot rush of air that blew the flicking shards of glass further away, into that black void. When she tried to move her legs did not obey, almost as if...they didn't exist. Roxie looked down, saw nothing, felt nothing.

There was no escape.

A scratch across her face brought her out of the dream, nightmare really, and back to the world in general. A gemstone glittered in the moonlight that filtered through the curtains in Lincoln's living room.

The topaz of the ring he'd bought for her. The one that matched the bangle he'd given her.

Shit, he was still gone.

She'd fallen asleep on the couch, waiting for news but nothing had come. With her eyes on the floor, she went to the downstairs bathroom and washed the makeup off her face. A glance in the mirror revealed bright blue eyes ringed with the smudges of exhaustion, as if a child with dirty fingers had walked in while Roxie was asleep, and tapped her beneath her eyelids. Shaking her head, she scoffed at the poetic thought and reached for her makeup bag.

Misery grabbed at her heart the minute she opened the bag and saw the lip gloss June had given her. June led to thoughts about Lincoln, and that nearly floored Roxie. She didn't put makeup on to please him, or anyone else really. Putting on makeup was something she loved doing because she created looks for herself that kept her real identity hidden away. Behind the makeup, her real self was an enigma, safe from onlookers who might question who she really was.

There was no point in adding the layers that would mask that person at the moment. Especially when a new idea sprang to mind. Darkness threatened to overwhelm her, she wanted to sit on the bathroom floor and cry until she could cry no more. That wasn't her way though, not when she had the perfect thing to help her cope, when Lincoln had created something out of what must be love for her. Even if he'd never said it.

She headed into the room that had been converted into a dance studio, changed into a black leotard with a gauzy skirt that came down to her knees, and tucked her phone into a pocket in the skirt. With earbuds in place, she set the song she wanted to dance to the most right then on repeat and waited for the music to begin.

An onlooker would see a woman dancing to silence, but the music was in her ears, filling her head with the somber notes of Beethoven's first movement of the *Moonlight Sonata*. Her feet moved by muscle memory alone through each step, with her arms up and over her head, as the music guided her steps and began to take the thoughts that haunted her from her mind.

There were things still left unsaid, things she needed to tell Lincoln, and the thought that she might never see him again was wholly unacceptable. It was more than just the things left unsaid that bothered her, it was an emotion she didn't want to define, despite everything they'd been through.

"I care about him," she said to the empty room, softly, just in case someone had woken up. "Do I love him?"

That was a thought that made her feet stop altogether and her arms came down at her sides. The reflection in the mirrored wall revealed a shocked woman, a woman too far gone to even know what she was feeling. In love? With Lincoln?

Old memories and new sped around in her brain and rather than face the truth, rather than admit it, she growled at her image and left to change into something less ballet. A pair of blue denim shorts, a loose sage green blouse, and a pair of blue deck shoes with no socks would be good enough.

"You're awake," June said as soon as Roxie entered the kitchen, unloading paper grocery bags.

Roxie looked over the black playsuit June wore, wondering if it was an indication of June's thoughts about what might have happened to Lincoln. For a moment, Roxie resented the fact that June wore a color more suitable to mourning, but let it go. June was her friend and Roxie knew that she often wore dark colors, even on happy occasions. Lincoln's half-sister didn't mean anything at all with the outfit.

"I'm awake. I tried to get some practice in, but I can't stop thinking about Lincoln." Roxie went to the fridge, grabbed some water, and took a seat at the table. "We have to get him back."

"And we will, honey, don't worry." June's voice, a shade deeper than Roxie's, spoke soberly but with conviction. "I'll give up every dime I have to do it if that's what it takes."

"I know you will." Roxie smiled faintly in June's

direction, knowing that all the money in the world wouldn't keep Lincoln safe from a drug addict who was too high to know what he was doing. "I can't believe this has happened."

"I hope you aren't thinking this is your fault somehow?" June asked, her voice sharp now.

"No, I'm not. I could, I know that, after all, this wouldn't have happened if it wasn't for Lincoln showing back up in my life. But no, I know this isn't on me." Roxie leaned back in the seat, her eyes on the ocean outside, taking in the peaceful morning scene. "This is so hard though."

"It's hard on all of us," June said, politely reminding Roxie that it was her brother that was missing. "I expect Mom will show up any moment now, but at least she's stayed away so far. I think she's in Paris at the moment, otherwise, I'm sure she and Dad would both be here."

"I'm surprised your dad isn't here, to be honest," Roxie admitted, turning her eyes back to June. "Have you updated him?"

"I have. He's working on getting the money together and he'll bring it here later this evening, I think. He may come here before that, if he can get the money together." June shrugged and started cutting up some of the strawberries and other fruits she'd taken out of one of the paper bags.

Roxie didn't bother to mention how strange June's

family was, she'd known that for years. Liam should be here too, June and Lincoln's brother, the one that Roxie had a crush on all those years ago, but he wasn't either. He was probably caught up in work or something. Or maybe he just wasn't close enough to Lincoln now to be worried. That was a sad thought but not unheard of in the world today.

Roxie didn't let his name leave her lips, she just watched as June sliced up cheese and added it to a plate that she brought over to Roxie.

"Eat this," June said as she sat down and picked up a slice of apple to chew on.

Roxie did as instructed and picked up a few slices of strawberry to eat. Chewing on the fruit didn't bring Lincoln back, but it did wake her stomach up. She ate a few more slices of strawberry, some apple, and a few squares of cheese until she felt full, and went back to staring out of the windows.

"We'll get the money, somehow, Roxie," June said, taking Roxie's left hand between hers. "We'll get him back."

"I hope so," Roxie replied, not sure of what else to say. She wasn't religious, or even superstitious really, but she didn't want to jinx anything at this point. Saying she knew they'd get Lincoln back without a problem was asking for fate to step in and smack them all with a dose of heartache.

After all, she'd known heartache time and time again since the day her parents died. That was why taking a chance on a relationship with Nathan had been such a big deal to her. He'd been so sweet, so kind when she least expected it, and he'd managed to fool her. Trusting Lincoln had been even harder to do after that experience with Nathan. Now, was fate about to teach her another lesson she really didn't want to learn?

If Nathan killed Lincoln, it would tear her apart.

"I'm going for a walk." Roxie pushed up from the chair and rushed out the door, unwilling to let June see the tears in her eyes. Or to hear the sobs that threatened to swell up out of her chest. Comfort wasn't what Roxie wanted, she wanted Lincoln back.

Her feet kicked at sand as she made her way to the waves gently rushing to the shoreline. She remembered the many nights they'd come out to swim in the water, how she felt safe from everything when she was with him. Except for her heart, maybe. That hadn't been safe from him for a long time.

Roxie sat down on the sun lounger somebody had left on the beach and brought her knees up to her chest. She'd tell him, if he came back, she'd tell him everything. Every little secret she'd hidden all this time, she'd tell him all of it. If she could find a way to put it all into words. And if he came back, of course.

Luckily, June and everyone else that came by the

house in the next hour left her alone to her thoughts. The sun started to burn her face, but she didn't care, not when the constant roar of water cleared her thoughts so well. She felt at peace for the first time since Lincoln disappeared, while she perched there on the sun lounger, listening to seagulls and the ocean that stretched across the globe.

Exercise hadn't done it and talking with June made it somehow worse. There was guilt mixed with Roxie's grief when she talked to June, guilt because the other woman was his sister and had to be feeling much worse about all of this than Roxie was. She wanted to comfort the woman, but she needed comforting too. She just didn't know how to do both, and get both, at the same time.

It wasn't possible, she finally decided. She'd have to be strong for June when she could be and take June's strength when it was offered. Anything else would be selfish and she'd never been a selfish person. Even if others had perceived her that way over the years.

But then the opinion of others had rarely bothered her. These people though - June, Emily, Kitty, and River - they all mattered, and so did their opinions. Roxie smiled, at last, thinking about how her friends had rallied around to help. Hopefully, there'd be news soon from one source or another.

So far, Lincoln's friend Kai had come and gone, as

had Tanya, one of Lincoln's personal assistants. Wendy would show up eventually, as would Emily. It was time to stop moping and see what else she could do to be of some help.

Roxie headed back into the house, kicking sand off her feet and swiping at her bottom to make sure she wasn't carrying any sand in with her. That was one of the drawbacks of living so close to the ocean, sand got everywhere all the time, no matter how careful everyone was.

"Any news?" Roxie asked June once she found her in the living room.

"Not yet, but that's good too, I guess?" June shrugged, looking helpless.

Roxie saw the dark circles under June's eyes, the tension around her mouth, and knew this was taking a toll on her friend. June had always adored her brothers, even when they thought she was just a brat. "I guess it is, in a way. No news is good news, right?"

"I hate that saying." June leaned back on the couch, her hand out to reach for Roxie. "Come sit with me."

"Of course," Roxie answered, taking June's hand in hers. "I miss sitting around with you."

"I miss so much about you." June's head swiveled to face Roxie, her eyes sad but somehow also happy. "I couldn't sleep for weeks after you left, even when my dad and Lincoln started to look for you."

"I'm sorry. I should have said something, sent you a letter or something. I was just so afraid of everything and everyone after that fire. I saw those men and well, my brain just went into disappear mode. Even when I saw Lincoln again, my first thought was hide, get away, in case him knowing where I was would lead those men back to me." Roxie shuddered to a pause, her eyes staring at nothing.

"Why didn't you go to the police, Roxie?" June chided, but Roxie shook her head.

"I heard what they were saying about my parents, that it was a murder/suicide, or that both of them had killed themselves. I knew they wouldn't believe an over-wrought teenager, even if I had some proof that those men were involved." Roxie shook her head, her thoughts on that night once more. "I can still remember how they both looked, staring at the flames that took my parents away from me."

"It must have been terrifying." June reached out for Roxie's hand again and squeezed it. "Maybe, once all of this has settled with Lincoln, it's time to go back and talk to the police at last?"

"Maybe. We'll see. I still don't have any proof that my father didn't set that fire." Roxie let her head fall back against the couch and looked at June with tired eyes. "It's not really that important right now, is it? I just want to get Lincoln back first."

"We will. My father won't let this guy get away with it either. He'll make sure he never comes back around again." June glared at the wall in front of them, her thoughts far away now. "If Lincoln doesn't kill the guy, that is."

"That is always a possibility." Roxie couldn't help but laugh softly at the thought. "He's threatened to do it so many times now, after this it's forgivable, isn't it?"

"I know the guy's an addict and not in his right mind, but still. They all think that what happens to everyone else won't happen to them, but it does so many times, and that addiction has destroyed that guy's life. It's sad, really."

"I didn't even know it was happening, at first. He hid it well for a while, but then he couldn't hide it anymore. Lincoln was so worried I'd be the one that paid the price, but it wasn't me. It's him. I'll kill Nathan myself if something happens to Lincoln, I don't care what happens after that."

"But I care," a male voice called out from the front of the house and both women jumped off the couch in a rush. "I care a lot."

2

Lincoln

Lincoln circled his sister and Roxie into a hug that he'd almost thought he wouldn't get to give. Both women were chattering, asking him questions, crying, and laughing all at the same time. Normally this kind of display would have him running for the hills, but Lincoln wasn't the same man he'd been the last time he was in this house.

This Lincoln wanted to hold and be held, even if it was only for a little while. He brushed June and Roxie's tears away, assured them he was real, and finally managed to talk them into letting him sit down. He sank onto the couch with a sigh of contentment. It was nice to sit on something soft and not a concrete floor.

"I'm going to go call Mom and Dad, and Emily, and

whoever else I can think of," June said and scampered off. Lincoln suspected it was so he could have some alone time with Roxie.

"I can't believe you're here," she whispered, wiping at her face with a tissue. She sniffled before she spoke again. "What happened? How did you get free?"

"I promised to pay that asshole what he wanted. I'm having it all put together now, as we speak," he answered, not going into detail about what he'd put in motion already. "I have a plan, Roxie, don't worry."

"But what if he comes back?" Roxie prodded, obviously not ready to let it go yet.

"He won't. Kai's working on it with Tanya, I promise. Now can I just hold you for a minute, please?" He pulled her close to his side, enjoying the smell of the sea and her perfume as she came to snuggle against his chest. "I'm home, and everything is going to be fine from now on, I promise."

"You promise?" She asked, and he knew that even if he promised, she still wouldn't believe it. Neither would he, if he were her.

He knew better now than to walk around as if he didn't have a single enemy to worry about. Of course, he'd thought he was protected, that nobody and no one could get to him because of the protections he'd put in place. Nathan had proved him wrong.

But that was for another day. Today he just wanted to be at home with the people that mattered to him.

"I'm going to leave you long enough to take a shower, change my clothes, and make myself feel human again. Why don't you order us some food?" Lincoln asked with a nudge. "I've not eaten properly in ages."

She narrowed her eyes at him and he knew she had questions. Her face cleared after a moment where she scrutinized every feature of his face. The questions would wait until later.

Lincoln hugged her once more before he left to trot up the stairs. He was about to collapse from exhaustion, but there was no way he'd let either Roxie or his sister know that. Getting away from Nathan had proven easy in the end, but the hours and days of waiting had taken a toll on him. Neither of the women downstairs had shied away from him but he knew he smelled awful. He felt as if his skin was about to crawl off his own body, he was so dirty, but they hadn't minded.

He made quick work of undressing, jumping in the shower, and lathering himself up twice, before he stood under the powerful flow to let the last remnants of his time in that storage building drift away. The last few minutes of his time with Nathan came back to him as he stood there under the hot water.

Nathan had stood near the rollup door of the storage unit, twitching almost uncontrollably. Lincoln stood strong, waiting, his eyes taking in the mess before him. A mess that used to be a man that Roxie cared about. Now, no traces of that man remained.

"I can end this, Nathan. Stop fucking around and let me put an end to this." Lincoln's words had been steady and even, despite the fact that his legs protested at being used.

"What do you mean?" Nathan replied, scratching at his neck as if he'd suddenly developed a bad case of fleas. "I want the money. I don't care how I get it anymore. I have to get out of here."

Lincoln smiled a victor's smile, knowing he'd won at last. "Give me a phone, let me go, and I'll arrange a safe place for you to go while I get the money you want in a truck that can't be traced to either one of us."

"And there won't be any funny business? You won't fuck me over?" Nathan's eyes wouldn't stay still but they did keep coming back to Lincoln. The man was at the end of his rope, ready to bolt. That desperation would serve Lincoln well.

"I won't fuck you over," Lincoln lied smoothly, his smile gentle now, full of compassion. "You'll get away free as a bird, no cops involved."

"Okay," Nathan said petulantly, as if he were a child that was finally getting his way after a tantrum, letting go of his anger slowly. When he swiped his wrist across his nose, he completed the image, and Lincoln had to fight not to laugh at how easy this all was. "I want it today, though. Not tomorrow."

"Whatever you need, Nathan. Can we get out of this storage unit and outside now, please?" Lincoln slowly walked towards the restless man, his hands out to show he meant no harm.

"Yeah, okay. Here, use this phone to do what you need to do." Nathan handed Lincoln a smartphone with a picture of a teenage girl with her arms wrapped around a boy on the home screen. He'd stolen it then. That didn't matter to Lincoln a bit, he just wanted to call Kai.

The smell of fresh air took his attention for a moment, once he'd left that awful room behind and he stood still, inhaling the faint scent of the ocean. It was good to be free.

"You can leave once I've made the arrangements, Nathan. Stick around for a minute," Lincoln said before he walked away for privacy.

"Listen, there's some information you might want. You can have it, for a price," Nathan had stuttered out, his eyes shifting back and forth, never still.

"What information?" Lincoln asked, never expecting the answer.

"It's about Roxie and a secret she didn't know I knew." The malicious grin on the thin man's face nearly chilled Lincoln to the bone. This man had once professed to love Roxie, but it was clear that had been a lie. Or it had become one as his addiction grew.

"Give it to me, and I'll decide what it's worth." Probably not a lot, Lincoln decided, but who knew?

"I'll give it to you once I've been paid. I'll email you." Nathan hopped from foot to foot, grabbing at his crotch.

"Fine, whatever," Lincoln answered, rolling his eyes as he turned away.

Lincoln sent a text message to a number he'd memorized long ago. The phone rang soon after and Lincoln answered.

"You okay, Lincoln?" Kai asked, his voice calm.

"Yep, I'm good. Send a car to me please, and arrange for a safe house while you're at it. Fill a truck with the money Nathan asked for and have it ready to go." Lincoln paused while Kai tapped words into a keyboard.

"Got a place, I'll send you the address. I'll have a car there in five minutes," Kai answered brusquely, always efficient under pressure. "Good to hear your voice again, Lincoln."

"And you, Kai. I'll see you at the house later." Lincoln ended the call and glanced at the phone to see that Kai had already sent the address. Good man.

"Go to this address." Lincoln showed Nathan the address and continued. "In three hours, a truck will be there, ready for you to go."

"Thanks, man. You're a lifesaver," Nathan sighed,

sagging into the passenger seat of the car he'd stood against while Lincoln talked to Kai. "I'll be so glad when this is over."

Lincoln stared at the man, wanting to punch his face in, but he wanted to see him in prison even more. A beaten face wasn't much of a deterrent. Nathan might come back and take Roxie next time. Prison bars would keep this broken man from coming near her again. Kai's connections in the judicial system would see to that.

"I'm sure you will be," he finally said, still fighting the urge to at least kick the man in the balls. Lincoln sighed in frustration and turned to watch for the car Kai would send. He didn't want to talk to the man anymore.

The car arrived, brought him home, and dropped him off. In the meantime, Kai was working on setting Nathan up. In another hour or so, Nathan would be in police custody, with a shedload of stolen goods, cocaine, and whatever else Kai could get his hands on hidden in the back of the delivery truck. Nathan would be riding away with a lot more than money he'd extorted, Lincoln thought with a smile as he came back to reality.

It was good to be home and back in control.

Lincoln dressed in a pair of gray lounge pants and a gray v-neck t-shirt then walked back down to find Roxie waiting for him.

"Your sister's gone back to the grocery store. She wants to feed you." Roxie stood up to embrace him in front of the sofa, her head falling to rest over his heart. "I can't believe you're home."

"I am, Roxie, I'm here. I'll never leave you again," he promised, meaning it.

He'd never been the settling down kind of guy, but Roxie had changed all of that. She was an enigma, a puzzle he couldn't solve, but he didn't care. If he spent the rest of his life trying to figure her out, he wouldn't mind a bit.

"Listen, there's some things I need to tell you," Roxie said, pulling away, but he put a finger over her lips.

Kai came into the house, disrupting whatever she might have said.

"I've brought you a new phone." Kai handed the phone over and put the accessories on the coffee table. "Everything's set up."

"Good. Thanks man." Lincoln meant for far more than arranging everything and the phone.

If Kai had burst into the storage unit with a group of men, they would still be looking for Nathan. This way, Nathan would go to prison for a very long time, and everything would work out the way Lincoln wanted it to. Lincoln was thanking him for waiting.

"No problem," Kai brushed off the thanks and looked over at Roxie. "How are you, Rox?"

"I'm good, happy to have him home." She put an arm around Lincoln's back and snuggled into him.

"I'm back," June called out as soon as she came in, her arms full of bags. "Lincoln, you need to eat, honey, and I'm going to make sure of it."

"Yes, Mom." Lincoln smiled, teasing his sister.

"You can mom me all you want, she'll kill me if I don't feed you." June glared at him but then smiled. "You're just lucky she's in Paris or she'd be here force-feeding you."

"Thank goodness she's in Paris then." Lincoln followed her into the kitchen, hunger now a gnawing pain. "What are you feeding me?"

"I thought pancakes with blueberry sauce, some sausage and bacon, and a few other things," June answered, distracted as she emptied bags.

"That sounds heavenly," Lincoln said and sat down at the table, the place they all seemed to be drawn to when anyone was here.

"I got sliced fruit and cheese for breakfast," Roxie said, teasing June. "It was nice, but I'd have preferred the pancakes."

"I'll make you some too. Sorry, I was distracted this morning, and slicing stuff up was about all I could manage." June took the sting out of the words with a smile. "I'd have preferred pancakes too."

Lincoln watched his sister prepare the mix for the pancakes but kept looking over at Roxie and Kai. Roxie kept touching him, as if afraid he'd disappear, while Kai watched with a critical gaze. He wanted to be sure Lincoln was alright, to see if he needed medical care, but he'd never ask Lincoln that. Kai cared, and that was all Lincoln needed to know for now. He was home, the only place he wanted to be.

3

Roxie

Roxie prepared for bed with shaky fingers. He was home, thank fuck he was home. Her eyes closed as reality hit her for the millionth time. This wasn't a dream about to turn into a nightmare, it was real life, and he was home. She glanced at her image in the mirror, noting that the purple streaks in her hair had faded, but she didn't care.

Her blue eyes sparkled in the light from an overhead lamp, her skin gleaming from the moisturizer she'd applied. It had been days since she'd bothered with that, but now he was back, and they could get back to regular life. She was worried he was so calm, but maybe reality hadn't sunk in yet? Would he have problems from his time in captivity? Would he have nightmares?

She walked out of the bathroom, determined to give him whatever he needed. Space, time, someone to talk to, anything he needed, she'd give it to him. She couldn't help but smile when she saw him on the bed, flipping through a menu screen of movies on Netflix.

"There's never anything worth watching once the new stuff has been watched," Lincoln said, obviously annoyed. He hit the power button and put the remote down. "I don't really want to watch anything anyway."

"I don't mind if you do." She smiled as she got into bed with him, sliding over close but not too close. "Whatever you want, Lincoln."

"I just want to sit here with you and talk about nothing." He grinned at her, his brown eyes full of mirth. "That's all I want to do."

She frowned for a second but wiped it away to smile instead. She'd promised herself she'd tell him all of her secrets, but now wasn't the time. It could wait, he just needed some peace for the moment. The things she had to tell him might just stress him out too much.

"I can do that." Roxie shrugged, but another thought made her frown again. "What makes you so sure this is over?"

"This." Lincoln reached for his phone and showed her the text Kai had sent earlier. "Nathan's already in police custody, charged with a mile of misdemeanors."

"What happened?" Roxie asked, her brows furrowed together.

Lincoln explained about the truck and went into further detail. "We have this protocol in place, Kai and the rest of us. Kai's parents started it when Kai was kidnapped when he was a teenager. Well, his parents put it in place, we've expanded on it since we all met when we were at university."

"Kai was kidnapped? How old was he exactly?" Roxie's brows couldn't get any closer together, but they tried. "I didn't know about that at all."

"It was when he was a teenager. His parents kept it quiet, out of the papers, paid off the kidnappers, and did the same thing we did today. They set up the kidnappers after they got their son back. Since then, we've all had a tracking chip put in here." Lincoln paused to show her the inside of his left arm, but she didn't see anything.

"A tracking device? But then, why didn't Kai use that with you?" Roxie was furious now and pulled away from Lincoln to sit up to glare at him.

"Um, he knew I wouldn't want that?" Lincoln looked as if he realized he'd made a mistake. He had. "Look, maybe Kai should have told you all that he knew where I was but…"

"But nothing. Motherfucker!" Roxie got out of the bed but turned back to glare at him. "He knew that whole time and didn't tell us? Fuck!"

"Roxie, I'm sorry. Please, don't be mad. I'm sure Kai had his reasons for not telling you."

"Fuck you," Roxie said and immediately cringed. "Sorry, that was too far."

"No, I probably deserved it." He put his hand out for her, but she didn't take it. She was still upset, but it was fading away.

She sat back down on the bed, her back to him. "I was so scared for you."

"I know you must have been, Rox, please, let's not fight. Not tonight." He pulled her towards him, turning to draw her in between his legs. She leaned back into him with a sigh, and let it go.

"I'm sorry," she sighed, and meant it. "I shouldn't be angry about things that happened before me."

"It's fine. I'd be mad too if I found out you were taken and could be found sooner, but nobody had done that." He paused for a second, then went on. "Well, that sounded complicated, but I mean, I know why you're angry. It's understandable."

"Well, at least I know if one of you is taken again, we can find you." She took in a deep breath and moved to face him. "So, really, tell me about what happened to Kai."

"It was back in China when he was sixteen. Some people knew he was from a rich family and they took him for ransom. If they hadn't paid, he'd have probably ended up sold off to a family without a child." Lincoln frowned but continued. "Since then, we've all watched out for each other."

"I can't believe I didn't know about that." Roxie tilted her head and put her hand out to touch Lincoln's jaw. He'd shaved and his skin was smooth, just the way she liked it. "Did June know?"

"No, but his parents told our parents about it later. They all put money together here and stashed some in the places we travel to, in order to make sure money was always available. June does have a tracking device, but I don't know if she knows that. Mom probably told her it was something else, knowing how Mom is with June."

"She's protective, but I don't think she ever had the same, I don't know, feeling towards June as she does you." Roxie knew June felt like she was never good enough for her mother, but that was a secret she'd told Roxie a long time ago. She wasn't about to share that secret, even if Lincoln was June's brother.

"Mom was always too hard on June, pushing her and pushing. I'm glad her father wasn't the same way." Lincoln moved back to lean against the headboard, his gaze inward now. "June's had it rough with Mom, but she's always had her father to turn to."

"She's lucky to have him," Roxie said, missing her own father now.

"She is, but I am too. He's still in my life, always there to support me, even if I'm not his stepson anymore."

"He always did seem very nice." Roxie's gentle smile was one of admiration for the man who'd taken on two sons that weren't his, but never treated them as if they weren't.

"He is," Lincoln agreed, his eyes on her legs now. "You have such beautiful legs."

"Thank you." She grinned and stretched back in the bed. "It's a shame you decided to go back to work tomorrow."

"Hmm, maybe I should stay home," he said, about to reach for her, but somebody knocked on the door.

Roxie grimaced at the intrusion but knew whoever it was wouldn't have interrupted if it wasn't important. She went to the door and opened it to reveal one of his PAs, Tanya.

"What's up, honey?" Roxie asked, her head tilted in question.

"Sorry, Rox, need to talk to Lincoln," Tanya apologized with a regretful smile, her eyes behind Roxie.

"I'll be there in a second, Tanya," Lincoln answered and got out of bed. He walked over to Roxie once Tanya walked off and kissed her cheek softly. "I'll try to make this quick."

"It's alright, I'll go get something to drink." Roxie

threw a white robe over the black negligee she'd worn to bed and laced it up. "Might as well hydrate."

"You may need it when I get back, yes." Lincoln winked before he disappeared down the hall.

Roxie followed him languidly, not in a rush. Her phone beeped in her pocket, and she looked to see a message from Wendy. She replied while she walked down the stairs, then headed into the kitchen.

"You're still up?" June asked, her eyes on a laptop on the kitchen table. She was typing something and didn't look up when Roxie walked in.

"Yeah, Tanya needed Lincoln for something," Roxie replied, not looking at her friend. She knew something June might not be aware of, and she didn't want to be the one to tell her. Lincoln or her mother could tell her about the tracking device. Roxie decided she didn't need the grief that conversation would cause. "What are you working on?"

"Just a paper I'm writing," June paused, frowned at the screen, deleted something, then typed a replacement. She looked up once that was done. "I'm going home tomorrow, but I need to get this done."

"Oh no, I hoped you'd stay a few days longer." Roxie sat down with a glass of apple juice and half-faked a pout. Most of it was real. She really did want June to stick around longer.

"I have to get back to my patients. Dad will lose his

mind if I don't come back soon," June answered, her lips flat as she shook her head. "I don't know how he ran that place before I came along."

"I understand," Roxie answered, leaning back in her chair. "I'm sure I'll see you again soon."

"You will, as soon as I can get away, I'm coming back. It's been too long since we've spent some time together where stress wasn't involved." June put her left hand over Roxie's right and squeezed. "I've missed you so much."

"I've missed you too," Roxie said with feeling, meaning every word. "It's been way too long since I had my BFF with me."

"I love you," June said with a sad smile, but Roxie soon wiped away the sadness.

"Not as much as I love you," she answered, the old reply that they'd always used back in the day.

"That was so long ago," June said after a brief silence, her eyes far away.

"It was. Another lifetime, another person ago, it feels like." Roxie shook her head, not sure if that was right. "I don't feel like Chloe anymore, but I know I used to be her."

"I think we all feel that way to a degree when we get older. The last time I saw you, I couldn't imagine being twenty-eight, it was so old!" June laughed; her brown eyes bright with joy. "What we didn't know, right?"

"You're so right. Holy moly, you don't know how right you are." Roxie's eyes sparkled but inside, a thousand memories came back to life, showing her just how far she'd moved away from being Chloe. That person was almost someone else, a stranger Roxie wasn't sure she'd ever really known. Years had passed and she was someone better in some ways, but there were things about her old self that she missed.

Like how innocent she'd been back then, how open the world seemed. Until the night her parents died, that is. That's when everything spoiled, as far as she was concerned, when the world became scary and dangerous.

"I'm guessing I do, in some ways, Roxie. For years I didn't know what had happened to you — if you'd been kidnapped, or just run away as everybody said. The police weren't looking for you, it was like they didn't care at all. I know because I went to them. They told me you were eighteen, not a suspect in the fire, and that you'd probably, um," June paused, her cheeks turning pink before she carried on, "had enough of deadbeat parents and left."

"How could they say that?" Roxie asked, seeing red as soon as the words came out of June's mouth. "My parents weren't deadbeats, they were wonderful."

"I knew that, but the cop I talked to said your dad killed your mom, of course they were bad people. I tried to tell him different, but he wouldn't listen to me." June's face grew redder, and her eyes became like two chocolate shards of ice. "I was so mad at that cop, but there was nothing I could do. I felt like the police were a waste of time, you were gone, and I didn't know why. I had to grow up quickly, too. Maybe not in the same ways you did, but there was still a lot that changed in the world when you left."

"I see what you mean." Roxie felt guilt crush her as she looked at her friend. For the first time, she understood fully what June must have gone through. "I'm sorry I did that to you."

"You thought it was necessary, and honestly? I understand now. You had to disappear, even from me. But I'd just like to say, I wish you'd taken me with you." June's tentative smile made Roxie grin.

"I wish I had too. But I don't think you'd have wanted to become an exotic dancer like I did." Roxie laughed, trying to imagine June doing a striptease. She couldn't.

"I'm stunned you did. Not that I'm judging you," June hurried to add, "I just can't believe you had the courage."

"I needed money and at the time, it seemed like a good way to get it." Roxie's shoulders lifted as if to say no big deal. "I was never really self-conscious or anything like that, although my first time on a stage was nearly my last."

Roxie laughed at the memory and June leaned over to ask what happened in a whisper.

"Well, I had to work there for a while, practice with some of the other dancers, wait tables, and stuff like that. I was so nervous about taking my top off, wondering what would happen, even though I'd watched the people in the club for a couple of weeks. I put it off as long as I could, you see. My boss told me to get up there and make some money or go home. So, I went up and promptly fell flat on my face. You see, I'd practiced, but not in platform shoes. I could barely walk in those things, much less dance." Roxie's laugh at herself mixed with June's and the house was suddenly a much happier place. "My boss was so pissed he nearly fired me, but I'd busted my nose and was bleeding, so I didn't care. He threatened to fire me again when he figured out there was blood on the stage. They had to shut everything down to sanitize the floor."

"That sounds like a nightmare to me." June frowned, but she was still laughing with Roxie. "I wouldn't have been able to go back up there."

"You didn't see how much money those ladies were making in tips. I needed money and that was the fastest way to do it, as far I could see. Now I make even more for half the work. I love it, really." Roxie took a sip of her juice and thought about how she'd helped River and the other new girls over the years. "If you can't do it, you can't, it's that simple. I came to find I liked it, a lot, and made it my life. I'd have loved to have done ballet, but this? It gave me life."

"I guess it's one of those things where you're either meant to do it or you aren't. I don't think I could have done it." June shook her head and Roxie let it go.

"It's not something anyone should be forced into, but it's lucrative. I've known college students, even university professors, that have done it to make some extra money. You'll see at some point, I don't always strip in my performances now, sometimes it's just dance and pole work. I do a lot of charity events for Emily and other people now."

"That sounds interesting," June said, her curiosity on display. "I'd love to see you perform. I always did admire your skills."

"It's a lot different from ballet, but I love dance, no matter how it's done. This is just a different kind of dance, really." Roxie picked up her glass again but didn't drink yet. "It's definitely adult entertainment, but it's not trashy."

"I can't judge you at all, Roxie, please don't think I am," June rushed to say, but Roxie shook her head.

"I don't think you do, it's just that a lot of people get all bent out of shape about it. I try to keep it classy." Inspiration struck and Roxie picked up her phone.

"Emily posted a video of my last performance on Facebook, here."

Roxie scrolled through until she found the video, a private video Emily had posted only for Roxie to see, and pressed play.

"Wow," June said as soon as the video started, her eyes glued to the screen. "You're so high up."

"Watch," Roxie said with an almost smug smile. She was about to drop halfway down the pole and come to a sudden stop, where she'd spin like a top. Roxie was gratified when June gasped and leaned in closer.

"That's amazing," June whispered absently, and Roxie's smile turned into a grin.

"It's easy when you know what you're doing. Muscle control and timing, that's about all there is to it." Roxie brushed off the compliment but felt pride in spite of her words. She worked hard to make that all look easy.

"No, it really is amazing. I know you know the technical side of it, but it's so beautiful. I didn't know it could look like this." June looked up with guilt in her eyes. "Okay, maybe I did think it was all about being over the top, but this is skill."

"Thanks, that means a lot to me." Roxie didn't want to say how much it meant to know her friend saw the beauty in her work, but she felt it.

"I'm finished if you want to get back to bed, Roxie,"

Lincoln called in to her and Roxie turned to see him coming in.

"Sure, June's just watching something on my phone, then I'll be ready."

He kissed her on the top of the head and went to the fridge to grab water. "I'll see you there."

Her eyes followed him, ready to be in his arms again. More than ready.

4

Roxie

Roxie slid into the king-size bed with Lincoln, reaching for him as need flared to life within. She needed to touch him, needed to feel how alive he was, to reassure her doubting brain that this was real. That he was really home and here with her.

Tremulous fingers danced over the silky skin of his back and up to his neck to plunge into the dark hair. Her hand came down once more, skimming over his side again, before going back up his spine. She moved closer, wanting to feel the heat that radiated from his skin.

Every part of him was silky to her touch, smooth and warm like satin. She loved touching him, learning every part of him over and over again. When he'd come back into her life after that long absence, she'd never expected to feel this way about him and hadn't wanted to at first.

Their first night of passion, a night when he introduced her to a world of sex she'd never expected to explore with him, had filled her dreams for the next decade, but she'd left him behind. She'd left them all behind, even Liam, the brother she'd had the real crush on. Lincoln had been an annoyance up until the night her parents died. Now, she couldn't imagine life without him.

She realized her hand had stopped moving when Lincoln turned to her and spoke.

"Are you alright, Roxie?" He asked, a gentle finger tracing the outline of her jaw.

"I'm good, it's just that I still can't believe that you're here," Roxie answered, her thoughts crisscrossing from one decade to the next.

He'd taken her virginity and she'd left the next morning. Now she wondered why she'd left at all. He was all she needed and wanted now. There was no other man that could take his place.

"I'm here, Roxie, and I'm not going anywhere," he answered as he moved the finger down her right cheek and along the column of her neck. "I will always be right here."

"Good. I can't lose you again." She moved her face up

to his to kiss him. She moaned in delight when his hand came up to hold her jaw still so he could kiss her as he pleased, deep and hard.

Desire exploded within her body, burning into life in her veins when he groaned into her mouth. Her tongue came out to dare him deeper, her right hand clutched tightly to his ass to hold him against her soft belly.

"Roxie," he whispered her name as he moved away from her mouth to trace a path down her body. She'd undressed before she slid into bed, so his lips met no resistance on their path down her body. There was only the soft sensation of them against her skin as he licked a sensitive spot here and sucked an even more sensitive spot there.

His left hand slid up her waist to cup her breast and her breath caught in her chest. He'd touched her nipples a thousand different times in a thousand different ways, but it didn't matter. Lincoln's touch always brought her body to life, excited her in ways she'd only ever felt with him.

His breath whispered against her nipple, and he turned the touch into sweet torture when he softly licked the tip. His breath cooled the skin, drawing it tighter.

"You always respond so beautifully," he spoke softly, his voice a vibration that she could swear she felt in the flesh trapped within his hand. "I love how you move against me, Roxie."

"I want you, that makes my body dance for you. I don't even have to think about it, my body knows what to do," she admitted, her body taut in anticipation of his touch.

"Hmm, I like that," he murmured and finally took the tip of her nipple into his mouth. His teeth captured the flesh. She gasped when his tongue brushed over the skin, then moaned loudly when he sucked the bud like a piece of candy that he rolled with his tongue inside his mouth.

Lincoln teased her until her hips moved against him frantically. She wanted him inside of her, to fill the emptiness inside with only him, but he pushed at her hip until she rolled back against the bed, his lips never leaving her breast. A gentle hand slid down her stomach, to her liquid center. Her heart raced when his hand moved to open her folds, to slide a finger inside her.

"Lincoln," she gasped his name, asking for more, but he didn't move, giving her the pleasure she needed.

He moved, but only to tease her other nipple while her hands clamped down on his shoulders. Roxie wasn't aware anymore of what she wanted. She only felt everything he did to her, felt the response his touch invoked, as another finger joined the first to fill her even more.

His palm pressed down into her, making her clamp

her thighs to hold his hand…right there. "Don't move it, please don't move it."

She didn't specify what, didn't care if she needed to, she could only think, don't move, almost there.

She tried not to moan loudly, they weren't alone in the house, but she stopped caring eventually. Lincoln's touch, his scent, filled her head and all there was in the world was him and her. Oh, and the exquisite sensation of his touch, that was definitely real too.

"Let it break, Roxie. Let the whole world break and just let go," he whispered to her, around the nipple still caught between his teeth. "Come for me, baby. Please."

It wasn't the fact that he asked that made her finally let go, it was the vibration of his voice, the way his fingers tilted just right as his palm drove deeper into that spot that finally made her do exactly what he'd asked.

She clutched at him, not wanting to let him go, but the world slipped away as a cry of pleasure tore from her throat. The sensation washed over her as he continued to move on her, continued to tease more from her.

She was on her way back to earth, back to him, when he moved, pulled back, and drew her over him. It didn't take much encouragement from him for her to impale herself on him. He wanted her, she wanted him, and the best way to ease that want was to take. So that's what she did, she took every inch of him inside of her body, wrapped him in sweet, liquid velvet that was nearly on fire for him and only him.

"I've wanted this so much," she whispered, her hands on his chest, bracing herself so that she could find just the right rhythm.

"I dreamed about you, wanted you so much, wanted to just smell you, Roxie. Fuck, don't stop." His hands clamped around her hips, holding her still despite his words. Lincoln thrust up into her, then decided that he wanted all the control.

With a single movement, he flipped them over and drove back into her, deep inside, where she wanted him most. Her legs wrapped around his back, pulling him deeper, tighter into her body.

She stroked his back as he moved within her, reveled in the feel of his muscles as he sought to give them both what they needed. It didn't matter whether she was on top or not, all she wanted was to be filled over and over again. Her hips moved in time with his, her feet now planted firmly on the bed to give back what he gave, to dance the dance that she would only do for him.

Roxie listened to his breaths, heard how they became gasps as he fought for control, her body responding with pleased satisfaction. Lincoln was about to lose it, and that was because of her. She smiled against his hot face, buried in the pillow next to hers as he thrust into her in a much tighter pattern, on the verge of letting go completely.

His skin was slick with his efforts, but that only made touching him better. His skin was hot, even his lips were hot when his face came up to kiss her.

"I fucking lo…, fuck, Roxie," he gasped out as she felt him lose it all at last.

She wanted to know what he'd been about to say, but let it go. She was too busy with the world slipping away.

Only when it stopped, when the world came back to them, Lincoln didn't roll away and leave her. He didn't fall asleep with a pat on the hip, he brought her up to his chest, held her tight, and didn't let go.

"I didn't know if I was ever going to get to feel this again," he said quietly, almost as if he didn't want her to hear. "I was afraid I'd never get to see you again."

"It's alright, Lincoln. I'm here and I'm not planning on going anywhere. Or letting you out of my sight for long ever again." She slid her right arm around him, clinging to him as her body calmed down. She felt the way he inhaled her scent in the way his chest expanded, loved the way he groaned against her neck.

His teeth nipped at the place just below her ear, pulling a moan from her throat while making her back arch at the same time. "Don't start it if you aren't going to finish it."

"I don't need the warning, Rox, I damn well plan to

finish exactly what I start," he answered, pulling her hips tight against his. He was hard again already, and she didn't mind a bit.

The pressure of his hand at her neck guided her to arch her face up to his for a kiss that felt as if it seared her soul. She was breathless by the time he let her face go and moved on the bed. He couldn't seem to decide what exactly he wanted as he nudged her onto her front to kiss his way down her spine. Then turned into a massage of her ass that nearly had her begging for so much more when he turned her back over and pulled her to the edge of the bed.

Lincoln knelt in front of her, guided her legs to open further for him, and proceeded to devour her. He used every weapon he had, an agile tongue, lips that sucked divinely, and fingers that knew just where to touch to elicit a response from her.

Roxie's hands scrunched up in the covers, her legs now over his shoulders, so close she could almost feel that first warning shock, but he moved again, standing up to turn her over onto her stomach. When he planted a hand on her back to push her down, she knew what to expect, but still gasped when he thrust into her.

The angle wasn't right though, and he moved his hands to tilt her hips, to guide her into just the right position to get exactly where he wanted to be. This time,

Roxie groaned long and deep as Lincoln's thrusts hit just the right place to make her see stars.

"Don't move, Roxie, stay right there," he demanded, taking more of the upper hand. She let him have it, knowing he probably needed this moment of control, this moment where he was the one with the power. If he needed to take his power back by pleasuring her, then who was she to complain?

Roxie took what he gave her, even when he clasped her wrists in his hand to hold her still. Her face pressed into the bed, so she turned her left cheek on the bed. She couldn't see him, but she could feel him, hear him as he worked to take her out of the world all over again.

His pace quickened when her breathing changed, when she felt a pulse of something deep and oh so good blossom into life within her walls.

"Lincoln," she whispered, but he heard her.

"Just let go, Roxie, let go and take me with you," he begged softly in return, his voice hoarse from his exertions.

He let her wrists go and dug his fingers into her hips to drive into her in just the right way, making her gasp as she went completely over the edge. Her right leg came up of its own accord, allowing him deeper inside of her, wanting to take all of him in and swallow him whole. She heard him cry out her name, felt his fingers dig tighter, just before she felt that first pulse of his explosion.

The room became quiet, except for the frantic sounds of their breaths as they fought for air. Lincoln had got what he wanted, but so had she. He pulled her up onto the bed, drew the covers over their bodies, and relaxed at last.

"I think I can sleep now," he sighed, making her smile in the darkness.

"I think I'll be in a coma in five minutes," she answered, her face pressed against his chest so that she could hear how his heart slowly calmed into a steady pace. She fell asleep listening to the reassuring sound, her right hand resting against his hip.

This was the most perfect place she'd ever been, and she didn't want to be anywhere else.

5

Roxie

"This place is really a good contender for your new club, Roxie," Keily said as she opened the door to a building a few miles outside the city. "I know it's not on the main strip, or even in town, but do you really want every Tom, Dick, and Harry walking in here?"

"No, that's a good point," Roxie answered, noting the entryway was just that. A cubicle off to the right with another, more secure door that blocked the path to the rest of the former nightclub.

There were three floors behind that door. Roxie knew from the photos listed on the real estate website that the first floor contained a bar, private parlors, a small kitchen for snacks and sandwiches customers might want, the stage for the dancers, and lots of seating. Behind the stage was the dressing room, a private office, and customer bathrooms.

"It's not bad," Roxie said as she looked around once Keily put a code into the lock on the door.

"I talked to the real estate agent this morning, she gave me the keys and the code since she had another appointment to get to," Keily explained, her eyes drifting over black carpet that wasn't suitable at all, but that could be changed.

"That's fine," Roxie answered absently, walking up to the stage to stare at it quietly.

Keily's all-American, blonde-haired-and-blue-eyed good looks made her smile seem even brighter as she looked up at Roxie. "What do you think?"

"I'll need to see the other floors, but this is good." Roxie hid her anxiety well and pretended that she wasn't distracted. She needed to have a look at this place and make a decision so she and Keily could move forward with their plans.

Worrying about what Lincoln was up to would have to wait. Okay, so it had been a week since he came home, and six days since she'd seen him. There was nothing to worry about, right?

"Let's go up, there's an elevator this way," Keily said, and Roxie followed her to a door she hadn't noticed before. The elevator was behind that door and Roxie got in when it opened.

"There are thirty-four rooms up here, although I'm not sure we'd need them all. The third floor is mainly two penthouses and quarters for staff, if we need that." Keily drew Roxie out of the elevator and down a narrow hall that took them to a much bigger hall with seventeen doors on each side.

"I like it." Roxie nodded, seeing that all the doors had security locks requiring a code to unlock them. "It's good."

Keily opened the door to show her an empty room but when Roxie walked in, she saw the room had its own bathroom. That was convenient. "That's great, they all have their own bathrooms?"

"They do, and some are bigger than others. The four rooms in the middle, two on each side, are larger and can fit king-size beds rather than queens."

"Good to know." Roxie nodded and headed back out to the elevator. "Let's see those penthouses."

"I think you'll like both." Keily had already seen the place the day before. Roxie had let her take over the search since it would be Keily and her husband's money that helped to bring the place to life. Keily was clearly enjoying every second of it. "I would love to have one of those apartments, if we didn't have the kids."

"That nice, are they?" Roxie asked, noting how Keily smiled with exaggerated need.

"They are! But they'll be great for you if you ever need a place of your own, or for VIP clients." Keily winked just as the elevator dinged and the doors opened.

"These are the staff quarters, even they're nice." Keily opened a door to show a room with a solid glass wall, obviously a living room, a kitchen off to the right, with a bedroom and bathroom behind that.

"Cramped, but not bad," Roxie said, and left the place, eager to see this penthouse. Keily closed the door and walked Roxie to another at the very back of a long hallway. Another door to the right would open to the other penthouse, Keily told her as Roxie walked inside the entryway.

A small hallway led to a living room and behind that were two bedrooms, a kitchen, two bathrooms, and a laundry room, but it was the living room that caught Roxie's attention. Another glass wall that gave a great view of the ocean in the distance. Not bad at all.

"That's nice but let me show you the rest." Keily drew Roxie's attention away from the view and Roxie followed.

"Wow," Roxie said looking in at the black granite island, countertops, and cabinets. The appliances matched the black theme and were brand new, as was the black marble sink. The bedrooms were empty, but the bathrooms featured deep, inset whirlpool tubs with shower stalls surrounded by glass. The walls in the bedroom and bathroom were also black marble and Roxie could see why Keily loved the place. It was tasteful, elegant, and so modern looking. "This is all really nice."

"See what I mean? I'd buy it just for this." Keily indicated the apartment with a wave of her arms. "What do you think?"

"I like it, it has potential. We'll need to invest in furniture and a lot more than I'd planned on, but if you're good with that, I am," Roxie answered, looking around one last time. "I think this might be it."

"I think it might be too, but there's a few other places I want to look at first, just in case." Keily grinned, and Roxie couldn't help but do the same.

"You're so funny." Roxie smiled and followed Keily as they headed back for the elevator.

"What do you mean?" Keily asked, her eyebrows lifted playfully.

"You know you want this place, but you're afraid something better might be out there. Take what you want, honey," Roxie replied, wishing she could take her own advice.

But that would mean acting like the crazy soon-to-be-ex-girlfriend when she pitched an absolute fit and demanded to know where the fuck Lincoln was. She tamped down on her fury and smiled at her friend. None of this was her fault, after all.

"Let's go back to my place, get some coffee, and have a chat, shall we?" Keily offered, her eyes concerned. "Something's on your mind, girl, I can tell."

"It's nothing really." Roxie tried to brush off Keily's concern, but Keily wasn't having it.

"Is it this place? Because the owner's background check came back clean, the place has never been raided, and the location is great. We still have the beach atmosphere outside in the private dining area where we can have outdoor events, but it's private, which we also need."

"It's not the place, it's great really." Roxie meant it as she looked around. Palm trees overlooked well-maintained grassy areas around the building and the parking lot in the back was well-lit. Any customers that visited could have a modicum of privacy when they stopped in to spend some time inside. Other places Roxie had worked at hadn't offered that and she knew that had lost the place many customers. Not everyone wanted their car hanging out outside a strip club for everybody to see. "This place offers a lot of privacy, security, and I like it if for nothing other than that."

"But you like the rest too?" Keily asked as she unlocked the car, her face anxious.

"I do, it's fine, really, Keily. Don't worry." Roxie smiled and checked her phone as Keily started the engine.

There were no messages except the usual reply from one of Lincoln's PAs, he was still out of town on business, but he'd be back soon enough.

Roxie let Keily do all the talking as they drove out to her house and even after. It wasn't until Roxie had a cup of coffee in front of her on Keily's farmhouse kitchen table, with Keily across from her, that she spoke finally.

"Lincoln's fine, I guess." Roxie shrugged, indicating she didn't know how he was really. "He's off on some business trip he didn't bother to tell me about, and his PAs won't tell me what's going on."

"But he's calling you, right?" Keily asked, her face full of confusion.

"No, he's not." Roxie looked down at her own hands instead of at the woman dressed in a pair of jeans and an emerald green t-shirt. "I thought when he came home that everything was about to change, that we'd attained some new level in our relationship, but so far? Nothing. I haven't even had a text message from him."

Roxie held up her phone before she wrapped her hands around the delicate china coffee cup decorated in pink roses. It was obviously antique, but Keily used them like they were everyday dishes. Roxie wasn't about to judge anybody right then, and lifted the cup carefully.

"What do you think's going on? Do you think he got spooked when he came home and felt overwhelmed about what he obviously feels for you?" Keily leaned back, taking a sip from her own cup.

"I don't know if it's obvious," Roxie started but paused when Keily gave her a look that cast doubt on that, "and I don't think he got spooked. I think he just… forgot about me."

"Let me tell you right now, honey, I've seen that man with you. He adores you whether either of you know it or not. Whatever he's doing, it must be important, or he'd call you. Maybe it's to do with his kidnapping?"

"I thought about that too, and maybe it is something to do with that. I don't know, he might have had to go out of the country again for all I know." Roxie took a deep breath to steady her nerves before she picked the cup up again. Her hands only shook slightly when she put it back down. "I just wish he'd let me know he wasn't going to be around. It's kind of rude, don't you think?"

"Well, yeah. You're living at his place, you're in a relationship, it's very rude. And kind of an asshole move too, but it's Lincoln. I'm sure there's a good explanation for it all. And if his PAs say he's fine, then he is. Now if he doesn't tell you what he's been up to when he gets home, then that's something entirely different." Keily's eyes sparkled with a fire that brought to mind how she'd once been a beauty queen. But that beauty queen had grown up to be one very determined lady who didn't take shit off anybody. "If that happens, kick him in the balls and burn his dinner."

Roxie laughed at that and when Keily winked, she laughed harder. "I needed that laugh."

"Well, it was only halfway meant to make you laugh," Keily said, a corner of her mouth lifted in a devious smile. "I halfway meant it as advice too."

"I understand, believe me. I've wanted to kick him so many times, but I thought those days were behind me. I can't believe he's done this to me." Roxie wasn't surprised how easy it was to talk to Keily about all these things. Something about the woman just invited confidences that she wouldn't have shared with anyone else.

Yeah, she could call June and complain, but Lincoln was her brother. She could call any of the girls she used to work with, but they were all busy with their own lives. Even Emily was busy lately, with all the charity events her mother had her going to. Emily had sent Roxie invites to all of them, but she didn't want to go anywhere without Lincoln. It wouldn't be any fun if she went alone.

"I guess I'd better go, the babies will be home soon, won't they?" Roxie said, knowing the nanny had taken Keily's triplet daughters out to shop with her.

"Yes, they will, but you can stay if you want," Keily offered but Roxie shook her head.

"I need to get back to the house and take care of some things myself." Roxie smiled and stood up. "But thank you for the coffee and showing me around the building. I think it's the one."

"I do too," Keily said and stood up to walk Roxie out. "And you're more than welcome to stay, I mean it. I'm making dinner in a little while, you could stay?"

Keily held out her hands and Roxie took them before she hugged the other woman. "You're an angel, but no. I'm good, I promise. I just need to stay calm until he gets back."

"Well, I mean it. Burn the shit out of his dinner if he doesn't have a good excuse." Keily laughed softly as she let Roxie go. "And if you need somewhere to land for a while, I've got an extra room."

"Thanks, I appreciate it." Roxie went out to the car she'd left here earlier and waved goodbye just before Keily closed the door.

She didn't want to go home; she'd be alone if Lincoln hadn't come back. She thought about inviting Wendy to dinner somewhere nice, but her friend had something going on. She was always busy lately, unless it was a phone call, and more than once Wendy had hung up the phone giggling and making very obvious kissing sounds.

Wendy must have found herself a lover, Roxie thought with a smirk. It was about time.

But that also meant Roxie was still alone when she walked into the house. It was obvious nobody was there by the absolute quiet that pervaded the place. Empty, the house screamed back at her when she walked into the living room. Every room was empty as Roxie checked, one by one.

Tears stung at her eyes, but she blinked them away and went to the kitchen to get a glass of wine before she sat down on the couch. Pulling out her phone, she ordered Chinese food to be delivered to the house and waited for her lonely dinner to arrive. There was still no word from Lincoln when she went to bed later, her dishes cleaned up and a load of washing in the dryer.

When Lincoln came home, she'd thought she'd never be apart from him for this long again. Even her bones ached, she missed him so much, but part of her was starting to get angry too. After what they'd all been through, how the fuck could he just leave her alone like that? What the fuck was going on?

6

Lincoln

Lincoln walked into the house to find it silent and still. The only noise was the slight hum of electrical appliances doing what they were supposed to do. He'd been gone for a week, stunned at what he'd discovered about Roxie while he was on that trip. It took him a while to let it all sink in, especially the fact that it was Nathan who'd told him about the whole situation in the first place.

He'd driven home with a seething, burning anger that made his knuckles white on the steering wheel. There was no good way to approach the subject, no way to make the truth disappear. She'd hidden one very huge secret from him and right now, that secret had broken him completely.

Part of him wanted her to be gone, to put off questioning her for a little while longer. But the other part of him wanted to get it over with so he could start to put this all behind him and get on with his life. That would be hard to do, knowing what he knew now, but he'd have to find a way.

A deep sigh was hidden by the sound of his footsteps as he walked up the staircase to empty his suitcase out. Instead, he pulled the case up onto the bed and unzipped it to pull out a file. Inside were written reports, documents, and photographs. Lincoln didn't open the file, he just picked it up once he'd changed into black lounge pants and a black t-shirt and went downstairs to wait for Roxie to come.

Roxie had some explaining to do.

Scratch that, she had a shit-ton of explaining to do.

He walked down the stairs with feet and legs that were tired, but he didn't want to have this faceoff with her in the bedroom. He wanted it in neutral territory.

Which was the main reason he hadn't called or messaged her. He wanted to see her face when he revealed what he knew now to be true. He wanted to see her expression so he'd know if she tried to lie.

Fuck, this was a huge mess and he didn't want any of it to be true, but it was. There was nothing he could do to change the fact that he knew this reality now, so he had to face facts. And make her admit the fucking truth.

Minutes passed, then a half-hour. Lincoln angrily got up from the couch and poured a measure of scotch before he went back to the couch to wait some more. Where the hell was she?

He knew from his PAs that she'd asked about him every day, even if she had stopped calling and texting him when it finally dawned on her that he wasn't answering. Maybe she'd left the house and gone back to her apartment, especially now that Nathan was in police custody and wouldn't be getting bail.

But then, there were still the people that were after Nathan to worry about. Kai had kept tabs on her while Lincoln was gone, to ensure her safety, but he hadn't said she'd gone back to her apartment. Maybe she'd gone back to that motel?

If she'd done that, surely Kai would have said?

Frustrated, Lincoln refilled the glass before he walked upstairs to check the closets. If she'd left, she'd have taken her clothes with her, and some of the other stuff she'd brought over. The scotch rolled smoothly down his throat, soothing the anger for a moment while he walked into the bedroom they'd shared for a while now.

The closet still had her clothes in it, and the bathroom cabinet still contained makeup, hair products, and straighteners. She was just out then.

He hated himself for the surge of relief that flooded

through tense muscles because he should be angry that she was still living here, not the other way around. He couldn't stop the sensation, even though he tried. He'd spent months falling for her, years even. Maybe he'd never quite got over the crush he'd had for her when they were both teenagers. Even though they'd hated each other.

Well, on his part, the hate was to disguise what he shouldn't feel. She'd been June's best friend, younger than him and still in high school when he was going through the college education June's dad had paid for. She was totally off-limits, even that one night they'd spent together. She'd needed him then, desperately, and he'd needed to comfort her. Sex was the only thing she'd wanted from him, so he'd given it to her.

Now the past was coming back to haunt them both in a way he'd never considered. Impatient, his heel tapping on the floor, Lincoln opened the file and looked at the stream of smiling faces in the pictures nestled inside. Some were new, some were old, all were printed from pictures found on social media.

Fuck, when was she coming home? He reached for his phone, thinking he'd just send her a message, but pulled his hand away. No, he only wanted face-to-face contact with her and he'd sit here all night if he had to.

He flipped to another section of the file; this one containing documents that had been secured for him by the private investigator. The documents shouldn't be in his possession, but that's what he'd paid the man a small fortune for. Proof.

With a grim frown, Lincoln started to spread out the documents, then the pictures, so that they made a nice little display. He glanced at Roxie's real name on several of the documents, remembering the girl he'd known as Chloe for the first time in a long time. She'd been so sweet, innocent, and very naïve. This wasn't entirely her fault, but what she'd done was still unforgivable.

Wasn't it?

A rattle of keys at the door made Lincoln turn his head and he stood up, the grim frown back in place. His heart twisted when he saw the way she smiled at him, her blue eyes shining in delight. He wasn't sure if it was hatred or dread of the pain he was about to cause her. It could be both, but he wasn't going to examine it long enough to make a decision.

"You're back," she said as she dropped the grocery bags in her hand and rushed towards him. "I'm so glad you're home."

Lincoln didn't say anything, he just stepped back and stared down at her. Even in heels, she was still short enough that he could look down at her. And she had to look up at him. Only the face that had been filled with delight a few seconds ago was filled with confusion now.

"What's wrong, Lincoln?" Roxie asked, blinking up at him with hurt dimming the shine in her eyes.

"We have to talk," he replied, holding his hand out to the coffee table where he'd spread out all the documents. "We have to talk about this."

"What is it?" She asked and stepped closer to look at the evidence he'd collected while he'd been away. "Lincoln?" Her voice shook and he saw the way her face blanched when she caught sight of the pictures. Her legs must have given out because she plopped down to the couch with round eyes and fear written across her face. "What have you done?"

"I found out your secret. Only, it wasn't much of a secret since Nathan knew about it. He offered me the information for a sum you truly wouldn't believe. I'd have gladly paid it, if he hadn't been on his way to sit in the county jail until his court date." Lincoln stood over her, unwilling to sit down beside her. Being near to her could be dangerous. "The thing I find incredibly unbelievable is not that you left photos around where that idiot could find them, where he could put two and two together. No, it's not that at all. What I find truly unbelievable is that you didn't tell me."

"Lincoln, I was going to tell you, but the time just never seemed to be right." Tears formed in her eyes as she picked up one of the pictures, a very old one that she was in. "I wanted to tell you the minute you got back, but you told me it could wait. I tried to tell you."

"But not back then, not when it mattered, right?" He spit the words at her, his anger getting the better of him now. "Not when I could have helped you."

"I was only a kid, Lincoln!" She stood up now, the tears gone, replaced by her own anger. "A scared kid, still a teenager, and homeless on top of that. What the fuck was I supposed to do? Ruin your life too?"

"No, you were supposed to tell me so I could figure out how to not ruin either of our lives. Maybe not run away in the first place so I could take care of you the way you should have been taken care of. Instead, you ran off and left me, to search for you for ten years. I can't fucking believe this." He strode over to the wall, his fist smashing against it as he totally lost it for a second. The pain refocused his brain and he turned back to look at her. "She's mine, right? There's no father listed on the birth certificate, but I assume she's mine?"

"Yes, she's your daughter. Can't you see how much she looks like you and June?" Roxie held up a picture of her daughter, one taken last Christmas, when Roxie went to visit for a couple of hours.

"I didn't notice it when I saw her, but yes, I guess she does." Lincoln brushed the words aside, his eyes still focused on her face. Watching for lies, for more subterfuge.

"I can't believe Nathan found the pictures. It must have been when he was looking for my mother's watch." Roxie looked down at her hands, at the ring he'd bought to match the bracelet.

"I wanted him to be wrong, Roxie. I really did," Lincoln sighed, turning away from her, not sure where to go. He felt too deflated to argue but the anger still simmered, hot and electric blue in his chest.

He'd expected her to deny it, maybe tell him that the cute little girl with her nose and the shape of his eyes wasn't her, their, child. Those blue eyes made it undeniable though.

"Wait, you saw her?" Roxie's head jerked up, her eyes round with fear again.

"Yes, why shouldn't I?? She's my daughter, I think I had a right to see her." The anger boiled up again, his eyes boring into her to deny him even that. "Of course, you decided ten years ago not to tell me about her, but that doesn't take away my rights as her father."

"That's why you aren't listed on her birth certificate, I didn't want you to be burdened with her."

"She's my fucking child, Roxie!" Lincoln shouted at her, pushed beyond belief. "I had a right to fucking know but you knew better, right? Well, you were wrong, Chloe, wrong about a lot of fucking things."

She flinched when he shouted, when he said her real name, when he glared at her with hateful fury. Her head went down again, but then came back up. "I did what I thought was best in the situation. Aunt Katie managed to survive that night and I found her at her sister's place. She took Lily for me, hid her from those men. Nobody knows she's mine, except for Lily herself and Aunt Katie. I had to hide her, Lincoln, don't you understand that?"

Her eyes pleaded for understanding, but Lincoln wasn't in a forgiving mood. "No, I don't understand that at all, Roxie, not when you should have contacted me. I'd have been able to keep her safe."

"If you saw her, then I guess you're right, in a way." Roxie paused to wipe tears from her eyes. "I must not have hidden her very well if you found her."

"Don't worry, I've got security looking out for her now. That won't be a worry." Lincoln pushed a hand through his hair, pacing as the anger fluctuated between explosive and controlled. "I want to see her properly."

"No, you aren't on her birth certificate, and you have no rights to her, at all." Roxie stood up, her face set in determination. "She's settled in her life with Aunt Katie, she's happy there. Don't go disrupting that peace for her."

"She's my child, Roxie!" He shouted again, not even meaning to, but how could he not make her understand that he wanted to keep the girl safe while being a part of her life? "You had no right to deny me that."

"I couldn't, oh, for fuck's sake, Lincoln, how many times do I have to say it? We hated each other back then. Okay, we had sex, but that was a one-time thing and it wouldn't have happened again. You were a grown man and I'd barely finished high school. It wouldn't have worked. It was best to just hide her with Aunt Katie and try to get on with life. I send money for her every week, I send gifts and I go visit when I can, when it's safe. I had no other choice at the time."

"But you did, Roxie, you could have called me. You could have told me what was going on and I'd have done everything it took to keep you both safe, whether you hated me or not." He didn't elaborate on the admission that the hate had been one-sided, he didn't want to go into that right now. "You never gave me a chance to help, you took all of that, everything, away from me."

He pictured her as she'd been back then - scared, anxious, broken in so many ways. Then he tried to picture her pregnant, with his baby, and something melted in his heart. He'd always wanted children and now he had one. One that she was still denying him.

"I can get a DNA test and force the matter. I can take it to court and get custody of her."

"You wouldn't take her from me." Roxie's eyes went wide as she gaped at him. "You wouldn't do that."

"Oh, you mean like you did to me? I damn well

would, Roxie. Believe it." He gathered up the file and glared at her.

"I won't let you do that," she said softly, but he heard the menace behind it.

As much as it might make him a dick, he knew she had little money. She wouldn't be able to fight him if he filed for full custody. Plus he knew a few judges that would be happy to help him out.

"Try me," he answered, a very dangerous smile in place.

The smile only faded when she grabbed up her handbag and left. He'd have one of his PAs load up her stuff and take it to her apartment tomorrow. For now, he'd done all he could handle for one night. He picked up the picture of Lily that he'd taken with his phone from a distance, and went up to bed. He had a daughter to get to know as soon as possible. The wheels were already in motion.

7

Roxie

oxie was…devastated.

That was the only word that came to mind as she left Lincoln's house and drove aimlessly. Yeah, she could head back to her own apartment, but she needed to be somewhere quiet, where nobody knew her, and she could lick her wounds in peace. Lincoln had threatened to take Lily from her, and that was what hurt her the most.

Alright, so she didn't spend every waking moment with her daughter, and she only saw Lily on special occasions. That was for Lily's protection, not because Roxie was shit at being a mother. Aunt Katie had looked after Roxie while she was pregnant and had helped her take care of the baby for the first few months after she was born.

It had been Aunt Katie that helped her make the difficult decisions about whether to put Lincoln on the birth certificate or not, and whether to take Lily with her when she left to go to South Carolina. Aunt Katie had always wanted a child of her own and Roxie was terrified of ruining the sweetest little baby the world had ever seen.

She was barely nineteen and needed to get on with her life, to make a success so that Lily could have everything she deserved. She'd made the hardest decision of her life when she left Lily with Katie that day and drove away. Every day since, she'd tried to make up for it in some way, but now it might all be in jeopardy.

If Lincoln filed for custody of Lily, it would hit the papers, back home at least. If he won, and Roxie had no doubt Lincoln had the money to do just that, then it would definitely be in the papers. And the men that had killed her parents would know that there was another Abshire out there to kill. One that would make Roxie very vulnerable.

That would make Lincoln vulnerable too, even if he was too angry to see that right now. She could understand why he was angry; she hadn't done herself any favors by floundering for answers. But the cruelty on his face when he'd announced he would take Lily from her had stung her deeply. Even now she felt an ache in the pit of her stomach that just wouldn't go away.

How was she supposed to deal with this? Should she call Aunt Katie and tell her to run away somewhere with Lily? Where would she tell her to go to that Lincoln couldn't find her?

Holy fucking moly, this was giving her the headache of a lifetime. She needed to stop somewhere so that she could focus on her thoughts properly. Stressing out while she was driving was dangerous. She pulled into a parking lot to stop for a moment and picked her phone up to call Wendy then decided going back to her place wouldn't be a good idea, even if Nathan was in jail.

There were still people that were after him for money. It wasn't safe there.

She could go back to the motel but couldn't really face the place right now. She wanted somewhere secure, totally locked down, where nobody could find her, not even Lincoln. A flick of her finger sent her contacts scrolling across her phone's screen. A smile crossed her face when she saw the name of someone that could really help her out.

"Hello?" A voice asked once she'd hit call.

"Hey, it's me. I need a quiet, secure place to crash for a while. You got anything like that for me?" Her voice sounded stronger than she felt, so at least she could still fake being okay.

"Yeah, I have a few, tell me where you are," the male voice said.

Roxie gave him the address where she was, and he told her another address to meet him at. "I'll bring you the keys and you can stay there for as long as you want."

"Thanks so much. See you in ten," Roxie said as she cranked the car back up and pulled out of the parking lot. At least she had a place to sleep tonight.

Roxie stopped and picked up a burger from a chain restaurant then headed to the address she'd been given. It was in the nicer part of the city, a place full of condos and high-rise hotels. She drove up to the parking garage, taking it slowly because the turns were fairly tricky as she climbed up the levels, but finally came to a stop on the top level. An elevator would take her to the condo she'd been promised, and she found it easily enough.

She knocked on the door and smiled when it opened.

"Hey, beautiful, how are you?" Nick asked, his eyes checking Roxie over. "You look good."

"Well, I was until a half-hour ago. I bought groceries and didn't even get to unpack them before all hell broke loose." She held up the bag containing a burger and fries that were quickly going cold.

"I'm sorry to hear that. I won't stick around, here are the keys. Stay as long as you like. I'm tearing this condo apart in six months, so you have plenty of time to get yourself sorted out before I do that." Nick smiled his charming smile and stepped out to the hallway. "Need anything else?"

"Nothing I can't handle myself. Thanks, Nick, you're a lifesaver." Roxie smiled back, hoping he'd go so she could break down and cry in peace.

Thankfully, he got the hint and waved goodbye to her. "Give me a call if you need anything else."

"I will," she called out as she closed the door.

Roxie walked inside the place and saw it was a small condo with a kitchen behind the door, a bathroom off to the right with a huge tub she would definitely spend some time in, and a living room just past the bedrooms. The main bedroom was a generic but tasteful affair done up in shades of light blue. Light pine bedside tables matched a dresser near the large closet at the foot of the bed. The bedroom was a bit of a squeeze, but it would do for now. The smaller bedroom featured a single bed, a closet, and not much else but Roxie knew she wouldn't need that room, so she closed the door on it.

The living room took most of her attention. It wasn't the large television, or the black leather furniture that drew her, but the sliding glass doors that led out to a large balcony. She could see the ocean from her couch if she wanted to. It was amazing.

Too bad her heart was too busy breaking for her to really enjoy it. She stood there with one panel open to smell the fresh air that blew right into her face. Her thoughts calmed for just a moment and she closed her eyes to enjoy it.

Roxie knew her life was like a train wreck sometimes and she knew trouble seemed to follow her, but this was just too much. After Lincoln's kidnapping, she'd thought smooth sailing was on the horizon. He'd come home and everything had been so damned good.

Then he left the next morning and she landed right back on that train speeding towards disaster. Only, she had no idea this disaster would wreck more than just her life. Lily would be ripped from the only home she'd ever known to live with a man she'd never known. And poor Aunt Katie, this would break her heart. She loved Lily like her own, and if Roxie asked to finally have Lily come live with her, a goal she'd wanted for a long time, Aunt Katie would follow right along behind.

That would be fine. But this?

Roxie's eyes opened, the blue a dark, stormy color, rimmed in red. What was she supposed to do now?

Give him time to cool off, she decided, and went back in to sit on the couch. Tomorrow, when he'd hopefully come to his senses, they'd work this out and everything would go back to normal. Right?

But what if it didn't?

The way he'd snarled at her pretty much told her there'd be no contact for a while. She needed her things from his place, but that could wait. Roxie was certain that one of the PAs would contact her about it at some point, but for now, she'd have to find something to sleep in and some personal products.

Picking up her bag, Roxie headed out for the nearest mall and bought some cheap pajamas, a few pairs of panties, some jeans, shorts, and t-shirts, and the products she needed to be clean and tidy, at least. She picked up a few groceries since the hamburger and fries were now stone-cold back at the condo and headed out.

Once she'd made herself a salad and eaten something, there wasn't much to do. As much as she didn't like to be around electronics, she'd gotten used to them while she was at Lincoln's. She turned on Netflix, filling the screen with thousands of choices. She settled on a series about female killers and watched it for a while, but her thoughts soon drifted away. Curled up on her right side, facing the television, Roxie thought about the things Lincoln had said.

Yes, she should have told him about his daughter sooner, but finding out she was pregnant had been terrifying at the time. There'd been no doubt she'd keep the baby, but how the hell had one night been enough? She'd been really naïve back then, and stupid too, it would seem.

Instead of calling Lincoln, she reached out to Aunt Katie. Aunt Katie hadn't asked too many questions, she'd just taken her in and given her a home after the most devastating event of her life.

Maybe she should have called Lincoln when it was time to give birth, but by then she'd put everything in the past behind her to focus on having a baby. She promised herself she'd tell him after the baby came, but by then she'd changed her mind again.

She chose Lily's safety over Lincoln's rights, and that's just how it had been. Yeah, maybe he could have taken care of them all, but he'd been trying to earn a degree. Roxie was sure his stepfather would have helped him take care of her and the baby, but there was also the fact that Roxie hated Lincoln.

Or did she?

She'd never imagined he could be as gentle as he'd been that night. She'd never dreamed it would feel so good to kiss him either. And part of her remembered that long after she should have forgotten him. There'd been dreams that tortured her, when there weren't nightmares. Dreams of being with him, of leaving him behind again, of losing her daughter in the mix.

It had taken her years to come to terms with her decisions, and then Lincoln came back into her life. Maybe she should have told him right away, but the time never seemed to be right. How was she supposed to just drop that on him?

Oh, you remember ten years ago when we had sex that

one night? Well, we made a baby and she's nine years old now. And she doesn't live with me. Want to meet her?

That wouldn't have gone down well, but it might have been better than how he'd found out. Nathan's rummaging through all of her things looking for that watch had revealed a truth she'd tried to hide from everyone here in South Carolina. It wasn't right that he'd tried to sell that information to Lincoln either, but he had.

Roxie really hoped Nathan spent every last second of his life in prison. You could only forgive an addict for so much, and Nathan had used up all the forgiveness she had a long time ago. She'd kick him right in the balls if he was in front of her right now.

Frustrated beyond belief, angry but powerless to do anything about it, Roxie got up and went to the kitchen counter. Peach gummy worms taunted her from a bag there. She glared at the treats and went into the bedroom to change into a pair of black pajamas before she snatched the bag up to take to the couch with her.

Gnawing on the treats didn't bring any kind of clarity to her, and certainly didn't send any answers her way, but they did distract her with each yummy bite. Until she remembered how she'd chewed through a bag of them the night her parents died. As well as all of the other stressful moments of her life.

What she needed was answers, but there'd be no

answers coming her way that night. Lincoln was royally pissed, angrier than she'd ever seen him, in fact. That was her own fault, she had to admit responsibility for it. If this broke them, after everything they'd already been through, she understood that.

But did that mean he had to take her daughter from her for good? Because that's what Lincoln meant. He wanted full custody of his daughter, and Roxie wouldn't have any rights to see her at all. Turnabout might be fair play, but she hadn't kept Lily from Lincoln to be malicious. She'd done it to protect them all.

It was doubtful she'd ever make him see that, though. He was so angry when she left, she knew he probably wouldn't cool off for a long time. Roxie chewed on her last gummy worm and stared at the television blankly. A woman on the screen was accused of killing her husband after she found out he was having an affair, but Roxie didn't hear any of it. Her thoughts were caught up on just how hopeless this situation was.

She could call June, explain things, and see if her friend hated her too. After all, Lily was June's niece.

Probably not the best idea.

Wendy? No, she'd been really busy lately.

Keily?

Would the former beauty queen offer to help her, or would she judge her for leaving her daughter with someone else? Roxie wasn't sure that would happen but moved on anyway.

Emily?

Also busy, with a family of her own to look after.

Which meant there was really nobody who could help her. Roxie was alone, again, with no idea who or where to turn to. At least that place was familiar, she thought, as she put the bag in the trashcan and went back to the couch.

Pulling a blanket over herself, Roxie closed her eyes and waited for the world to just disappear and leave her alone.

8

Lincoln

"Hey, big brother, how are you?" June's voice banged into his head like a hammer on speed.

"What? What time is it?" Lincoln asked, sitting up in bed, his eyes clamped tightly shut against any light that might be in the room.

Hungover wasn't even the word for the way he felt right now.

He'd finished an entire bottle of scotch after Roxie left the night before, so the hangover wasn't a surprise. What was a surprise was that June was in his bedroom.

"I came over to spend some time with Roxie, but she's not here. Where is she?"

"I don't fucking know, June. Please, speak quieter."

Lincoln put his palm to his left temple and grimaced. "Please speak quieter."

"What's going on?" June walked closer, apparently close enough to smell the scotch fumes because she frowned and took a step back. "What have you done?"

"I found out the truth. A truth I should have been told ten years ago but Roxie decided I didn't need to know." Lincoln didn't care if that made any sense at all. He wanted a shower and coffee.

He wasn't surprised to find himself dressed in yesterday's rumpled clothes, and peeled the shirt off as he got up from the bed. The shirt was discarded as he headed for the bathroom.

At least June said the only words he wanted to hear as he walked away.

"I'll make coffee."

She was an angel.

The shower cleared his head a little, but the pain only throttled back slightly. The problem seemed to be his stomach was upset too and the pain in his head was making it so much worse. And none of that touched the ache in his chest.

With his right hand on the shower wall, his head under the thrumming pressure of hot water, Lincoln remembered the first time he laid eyes on his daughter. Something broke in him, a wall he hadn't known was up around his heart. He'd loved her the instant he saw her, even if that sighting was from a non-threatening distance.

And amongst that love was anger -, dark, malicious anger. Roxie had lied to him. She'd looked him in the eye on so many occasions with innocent eyes, not telling him the most important secret of all. A secret that could have changed the world for him a long time ago.

The second he set eyes on Lily everything had changed, and Lincoln knew that if Roxie, Chloe back then, had told him about the baby he'd have been someone completely different. He might even be a better man than he was now.

There'd have been no anger about the fact that she got pregnant, he was the stupid one who didn't make sure to use a condom. He could have protected her all these years.

But maybe she hadn't wanted to be protected. That thought intruded into his brain and he turned the water off.

She was fiercely independent; she really didn't need someone to take care of her. Protection was different, as far as he was concerned, but she hadn't needed him for anything, really. Any number of her friends would have found a place for her to hide, if he hadn't been here now.

But he'd have liked to have had the opportunity to be a father to Lily and a protector to Roxie. To the girl he'd known as Chloe, he reminded himself. The woman was Roxie. Chloe didn't exist anymore.

He went downstairs after he put on fresh pajamas, to find June had made coffee and toast. He took portions of both and joined her at the table.

"What's going on, Lincoln?" June asked, sliding two Acetaminophen over to him.

Lincoln took the pain relievers gratefully, gagged them down with a swallow of coffee, and looked at his sister as if to judge how she'd take the news he had to give. After another sip of coffee, the decision was made.

"Ten years ago, I helped Chloe escape." He couldn't remember now if he'd ever admitted that to her, his brain hurt too much, but he knew the next part had remained a secret. At least, on his part. Roxie might have told her, but Lincoln knew he had never told a soul. "We were also, ahem, intimate that night."

"Intimate?" June's arched left eyebrow just added more doubt to the tone in her voice. "You and Chloe? You and Chloe who hated each other were…intimate?"

"Yes, June. *Fuck.*" He put the empty coffee cup down and glared at her. "Why's that so hard to believe?"

"Well, Lincoln, you *hated* each other, that's why." June sat back in her chair, her face twisted in doubt, but the doubt cleared away after a moment. "Okay, it doesn't matter if I believe it or not, why is that important?"

"It's important because she got pregnant that night.

And had a baby. And didn't tell me a fucking word about it." He looked at her, watching for her reaction.

June's pretty face twisted from disbelief to surprise, and then to understanding. "Oh. Fuck."

"Yes, oh, fuck." Lincoln gnawed at a piece of toast, tasting none of it, but he knew he needed food.

"What did she do with the baby?" June asked gently.

Lincoln knew it was because June was the one person who knew how much he wanted children. He'd never wanted a wife, but a warm home filled with the sounds of family and happiness? Yeah, he really wanted that. "The woman who worked at the house has our daughter."

"Aunt Katie?" June asked, clearly surprised. "I thought…well, I don't know what I thought. I never heard about her again, so I assumed she'd moved on or something."

"She did, with my baby." Lincoln's anger was creeping up again, he needed to get it under control.

He looked around the kitchen that Roxie had decorated perfectly, choosing the colors he'd have chosen. There were pieces of her all over this house, things that showed how much she cared and wanted his comfort. But all the time she was decorating his house, letting him fall for her, she was holding back one very important secret.

"I confronted her about it last night, and she gave me

a bunch of excuses about how she'd been terrified for the baby, that she was young and didn't know what to do, some other stuff about how she didn't want to ruin my life." Lincoln's words trailed off, uncertainty entering in, now that he'd had time to think about it all.

Of course, he'd spent the night very drunk, but he'd still been able to retain a few thoughts. Everything she'd told him had been a confession of how she'd wanted to protect him or the baby, not herself. She hadn't said she didn't want to be saddled with a baby; it was all about protection. That was, well, kind of understandable in the cold light of morning.

"And what did you say that made her leave, Lincoln?" June asked carefully, her eyes watching him closely.

"That I was going to file for custody of Lily. That I was going to take our daughter from her." Lincoln closed his eyes and pinched the bridge of his nose where the pain seemed to have decided to take up residence and throw a party.

"That's fucked up, Lincoln," June said, disappointment in her eyes. "She's been through so much already. And how did you find out about the baby anyway?"

"Nathan told me, sold me the information. He'd found some pictures when he was tearing Roxie's place apart..." Lincoln let the words trail off. June's point was made with that sentence.

"You have a right to be angry, Lincoln, but surely you

can see what she was going through. Has been going through? She nearly fell apart when you were missing. I've never seen her that lost, and the day after you came back you ran off and left her alone again. Then, then, oh fuck me, Lincoln, you're more of an asshole than I'd have ever believed," June paused, looked like she was about to be sick, but went on. "Then you came back and unloaded on her about something that must have terrified her even more, something that must have nearly broken her. I can't believe you."

June got up, put her dishes in the sink, and then stood there glaring at him.

"Right, you would take her side." Lincoln twisted out the verbal knife she'd stuck into his chest with her words and threw it back at her. "She's your best friend. I'm your fucking brother, but you'll still take her side."

"No, Lincoln, that's not what I'm doing at all. I'm seeing the truth, I'm seeing what you've both been through, and wondering why the fuck you chose to attack her with that weapon when you know the kind of trauma you've both experienced. Because that's what you did, you attacked her. No wonder she left. Fuck. I can't believe you."

Lincoln tried to break into the stream of his sister's anger, but she held up a hand. "No. You're one to talk about secrets, anyway. Have you forgotten how you've tracked her all these years? Have you told her about that? Or what you found out about her parents? Have you told her any of that? Because she hasn't said anything about it to me. Have you told her how Dad told us not to believe the news because none of it was true?"

Lincoln didn't look at her, didn't want to admit he'd totally put all of that off. Or that he was still working on that case with his PI.

June scoffed at him before she left the kitchen and a few seconds later Lincoln heard the front door close.

Now June was mad at him too. For fuck's sake.

Lincoln put his dishes in the sink and went back to bed.

June was right with that last parting shot; he should have told Roxie what he'd found out so far. Roxie had a right to know. But he had a right to know about his child. She'd kept that from him. Now, she wouldn't know because she most definitely was never going to speak to him. He'd made sure of that with that threat he'd made.

The darkness of the room had always been perfect. Roxie had known somehow that he wanted only oblivion when he went to bed. There was a television, but nothing else to serve as a distraction. The blackout curtains kept it dark, even during the brightest parts of the day. He retreated there now, not to think about what June had said, but to try to block out the image of

Roxie's face when he'd flung that sentence at her. That was the ultimate violation.

She'd been through nothing but hell since that night. Okay, there might have been some good years here and there, but he knew the last few months had been nothing but a blunder from one trauma to the next. She'd handled it all with bravery, a courage he'd admired. Then, when it looked like most of it was over, when it looked like there might be some peace on the horizon, he'd let the last little trump card that Nathan held tear them apart.

Whether it was a mistake or not he didn't know. He was still too angry to think about anything but how she'd betrayed him when she didn't tell him about their child. The image of her betrayal kept intruding, wouldn't let him rest, no matter how many times he turned in the bed, no matter how many times he punched the pillow.

The biggest mistake was pulling her pillow close to him to brace his arm on. It smelled of her shampoo, her perfume, the essence of her scent lingering to torment him further.

"Fine, I'll get up," he said to the otherwise empty room. He sat on the edge of the bed, staring into the darkness.

The smell of Roxie wouldn't leave him alone, so he got up, angrily snatching at the bedding, pulling at the pillowcases until he nearly tore one. With rushed steps, he went downstairs to the washer and threw everything inside. When that was done, he went back up to the linen closet to pull out fresh bedding.

New bedding took away her smell, sure, but not his memories of her in that bed. Lincoln stared down at it and wondered if he'd ever be able to sleep in it again if he was sober. It was too early to start drinking and he needed something more substantial in his stomach than toast if he was really going to drink himself into a stupor again tonight.

What if he was wrong?

That question gnawed at him while he drove out to get some food. It plagued him as he put each tasteless bite of whatever it was that he'd ordered into his mouth. And later, when he sat staring at the churning ocean, as angry as he'd felt yesterday, sipping at a brand-new bottle of scotch, he questioned again. What if he was wrong?

Did two wrongs make a right? She'd not told him about Lily. She had her reasons. Were those reasons enough? Especially now, when she knew he could protect the girl better than anyone else could. His PI found her quite easily, therefore anybody could, if they knew about her. Roxie might have thought the girl was safe, but she wasn't, and that was the simple truth of it.

Another measure of amber liquid filled the glass, the

top off the bottle to make refilling easier, and Lincoln drank again. His phone was off, the doors were locked, and he'd dragged one of the recliners over to the window in the kitchen, so he could stare out at the rain-drenched scenery outside. The storm was a surprise, but he hadn't really paid attention to much of anything since June left. Lightning flashed, filling the world with brilliant white light.

The flashes pierced into his brain each time, but the alcohol was already at work, numbing everything but the deep empty ache in his gut. That wasn't a hunger for food, or for the child he'd yet to meet. It was a feeling of loss.

Somehow he couldn't turn off what he felt for Roxie. He couldn't tell himself to stop loving her, needing her, despite the seething anger that boiled beneath the surface. He was royally fucked now, he decided, taking another sip. No matter what he did, he was fucked. So where did that leave him?

9

Roxie

oxie woke up to the sound of the ocean, but it wasn't right. She shouldn't be able to hear the ocean from Lincoln's bedroom. She frowned before she opened her eyes. Reality came flooding back in as the dark sky outside came into view.

That's right. She wasn't at Lincoln's house; she was at one of Nick's places.

Hiding.

From Lincoln.

Not out of fear, but because she couldn't be anywhere he could find her.

He was too angry with her, too hurt, and the pain of knowing he was that upset with her was one of the worst hurts she'd ever felt. Nothing would ever trump losing her parents, or leaving her daughter with Aunt Katie, but this? This was a different kind of hurt.

She'd spent most of the day lost in thought, to the point she'd ignored her phone. Then she'd fallen asleep. Something woke her up.

A stronger knock at the door than the one that woke her sounded. Roxie knew it had to be Nick, nobody else knew where she was.

She was still dressed in last night's pajamas, but it didn't really matter. She had a bra on, that was all he was getting as far as being properly dressed went.

He smiled, obviously relieved, when she opened the door. "Hi, I'm so glad you answered the door finally. I've been trying to call you all afternoon."

Nick was tall, really fucking tall, at six foot five inches, and slim, but not in a way that made him look like a beanpole. Rather, he had a broad chest, deep blue eyes that were certainly good enough to drown in, and silky blond hair. He was a god amongst men, but not what Roxie wanted. She wanted Lincoln, even if that was done and over with now.

"Sorry, it's been a shitty day for me." She opened the door to let him come in and closed it behind him. "I turned my phone off, and I've been asleep."

"I didn't mean to wake you," he said softly, walking to the small table in the kitchen to take a seat. "Are you hungry? I can order something."

"No, I'm good." She brushed the offer off and sat with him. "I think there's some coffee if you want or some tea?"

"No, I'm good, too. I mainly just wanted to check on you, Roxie. What's up?" He leaned back in the chair, at ease, but then he should be, this was his place.

"Things aren't great with Lincoln." She hated to admit it, she'd gone running to Nick once before and made a fool of herself. She wouldn't make that same mistake again. That connection wasn't there, and Nick was the marrying kind. Handsome he may be, but she wasn't looking to marry him. "I hid something from him, that I obviously shouldn't have, and well, now that's bit me in the ass."

Nick, as always, was gentle, and not pushy at all. "Was it something that he needed to know?"

"I didn't think so at the time, but yes, I should have told him. I thought I was doing what was best for all involved, but it seems not."

"Well, it's like this my lovely, you weren't born with the name Roxie, but that's not important to me. And no," he said quickly, when she started to speak, "I don't need to know if I'm right or not. You have your reasons, and that's all that matters. But if that's what he's upset about, then he needs to get the fuck over it."

"It's not. It's something much bigger." Roxie debated telling him, and he waited to see if she would, but she shook her head. "I can't tell you right now. But he's totally justified in hating me."

"Hate's a strong word," Nick said, considering her with narrowed blue eyes, so much colder than her own. "Are you sure he hates you?"

"I think he did by the time I left yesterday, yes." She nodded for emphasis, her eyes bouncing from his to the wall behind him. She didn't want to put Lily in any more danger, and although Nick was probably one of the safest people she could tell, she wouldn't take that chance even with him. "Thank you for not pushing me for an answer."

"Roxie, you've always been your own woman. You know your mind, and I still think if you hid something from him, you had your reasons. Whether they were justified or not, I guess is up to him, but I know you. You wouldn't hide something if it wasn't important to do so." His eyes bored into her now and she realized, not for the first time, just how much he cared about her. If only she could love him, life would be so simple. She could get Lily, find a home for them all and live a life of luxury.

But the only love would be what she had for her daughter.

Nick deserved more than that from a wife.

"I thought it was important at the time. Very important. And I kept meaning to tell him, but the moment was never right," Roxie sighed and got up for a glass of water. "I know he didn't mean to keep brushing off the moments when I said I wanted to talk, or when I said I needed to tell him something, but, well, it's been one hell of a ride lately. We've not really had time to do more than breathe. Well, until yesterday. It all came out, and he was not happy."

"I'm still sure you had your reasons." Nick crossed his arms over that very broad chest of his and gazed at her levelly. "You aren't a malicious person, Roxie. You're actually very giving for someone who's had to take all the shit you've had to take lately."

"You don't know the half of it," she muttered, but he heard her.

"Then tell me?" He asked, it wasn't a demand.

"My parents died in a fire when I was a teenager. It really ruined my childhood, and all those early years of my adult life were colored by it. I didn't have someone to run home to, or parents that could bail me out of trouble. I was on my own and whatever decisions had to be made, I made them."

"Ah, that's why you've always been so independent." He nodded as if things made sense now.

"Pretty much, yeah. I had to hold my own hand so many times that I got used to it. Nathan really fucked me up when he ghosted me that first time. I thought he was different. Then I became involved with Lincoln, and well, that's a shitshow that I can't explain a lot about." Roxie sat back down and looked at Nick.

He didn't look upset or bothered by anything she'd revealed so far. Would he help her if she asked?

No, she couldn't take advantage of him like that. He'd do it because he adored her, no matter what it cost him, and it might cost him far more than money. She couldn't put him through that. She'd have to save every penny she had and fight Lincoln for her daughter, if it came down to it.

But would it really be such a bad thing?

Lily deserved to know her father and Lincoln did have a lot of money to provide the kind of security Lily would need to protect her.

Not at the cost of never seeing her daughter again, though. That was a price she was unwilling to pay.

"How can I help, Roxie?" His eyes implored her to tell him anything she wanted, but she didn't have an answer.

"You've given me somewhere to hide for a little while. That's the best gift you could give me. I need time to think, to plan a strategy, and I can do that here."

"Are you sure that's all?" He didn't seem convinced that was all he could do.

"I can't think of anything else, Nick." She laughed softly, shaking her head. "If I think of something, you'll be the first to know. I promise."

"Good. Now, are you sure you won't want dinner? I can take you anywhere you want to go or call somewhere and order in?" He held up his phone, but she shook her head no.

"No, I'm not hungry. I ordered Chinese earlier." She hadn't but he didn't need to know that. She'd had a sandwich, and that was enough for today.

"Okay. Can I sit out on the balcony with you for a while then? I could use some company, if you can stand me." Nick let his façade of easy-going nonchalance slip for a moment, and Roxie just couldn't say no.

"Sure, what's up?" She got up and they walked out to the balcony. At least the rain had stopped at some point. A quick check showed the brown wicker furniture was dry before they sat down.

"Nothing much, I've just been running on empty for a while and need a break." He sighed but held a hand up. "Don't worry, I'm going on vacation next week. I'm going to Germany for a week."

"Oh wow, lucky you!" She smiled over at him across the square glass table that separated them. "I'd love to go there."

"I could take you with me? No strings attached." He smiled at her invitingly, but Roxie knew there were always strings attached. Of some kind.

"No, I've got things to sort out here before I take off for a week." She shook her head with regret but knew it was for the best. A trip like that would only cause her more problems in the end.

They sat quietly for a while, watching the surf crash and pound the shore. Nick made motions to get up after a while and excused himself. "I need to get back home and get to bed. It's late."

"Thanks for stopping by, Nick. I'm fine and will be, I promise." Roxie brushed at his elbow with her hand and smiled. "It really will."

"I hope so, for your sake. I only want what's best for you, you know?" He looked unhappy for a second before his face cleared. "No matter what you do, or who you end up with. I just want to see you happy, Roxie."

"Thank you, Nick. I wish the same for you." Even if that meant she lost his friendship to some woman who wanted him all to herself. It would only be fair, she decided, he deserved a woman that wanted all of him.

"Take care, Rox, I'll see you before I leave." He waved goodbye, and she closed the door.

Roxie went to the couch and slumped down beneath a cover. The breeze was a little cool and she should close the door, but she liked smelling the salt in the air. It reminded her of being at Lincoln's. Which wasn't the smartest thing to remind herself of right now but fuck it. Why shouldn't she drown in her misery? She was a grown woman, her bills were paid, for this month anyway, and she'd just been brutally...dumped?

That had to have been him breaking up with her. There was no point denying it, even if she wished it was all different. If he'd only let her tell him when he came home, but he hadn't. She'd wanted desperately to tell him about Lily that night, but he wouldn't have it.

Which reminded her.

Roxie picked up her phone and dialed a number.

"Hello?" Aunt Katie asked, a smile in her voice. "How are you, Roxie? Everything's calmed down, I hope?"

"Kind of, but mostly no," Roxie said with a frown. "Lincoln found out about Lily. He wants custody of her."

"I see," Aunt Katie said softly, and Roxie could just imagine the older woman biting her lip in worry. She always did that when something bothered her.

"Yeah, it's not good. He has the power and the money to do just that. I don't know what to do," Roxie said to Katie for the millionth time in her life. Aunt Katie was the only one she'd had to turn to when she lost everything. To her credit, Aunt Katie never complained.

"We'll do what we have to, what we must, honey, as we always do," Aunt Katie answered using the comforting pet name. "We can't fight a man or a family as powerful as they are. We'll just have to try and fight for what we can."

"I know. I'm just afraid of him taking her from you, of never seeing her again," Roxie said the words she'd never expected she'd have to say.

If Lincoln had just let her tell the truth that night none of this would have happened. He'd insisted however and that had been a mistake for all of them as it turned out. "Part of me wants to tell you to pack a bag and I'll come get you both. We could run for Mexico. He'll have to find us first, demand a DNA test, and then file for custody."

"You know that will only make things worse, honey. No, we have to stay here and face the music. Lincoln isn't a bad man. He'll come to his senses once the anger has eased a little. He knows you're her mother. She loves you and taking her from you permanently will only make her hate him. I'll tell him that myself if it comes down to it." Aunt Katie might be sensible, and loving, but she wasn't a total pushover. She just knew what common sense was and what wasn't.

"I guess you're right." Roxie didn't want to admit it, but that was the truth. She was going to lose custody of her daughter, but not right away. "For now, we'll leave things as they are. I may come up there, I'm not sure yet. I'm still hoping there might be a way for me to fix this. I don't know how, but I'm hoping."

"If anybody can do it, it's you, honey. I have faith in you."

"Thank you, Aunt Katie. Kiss her goodnight for me." Roxie knew it was already past Lily's bedtime, but she also knew Aunt Katie would do just that.

"I will, honey. Good night." Aunt Katie hung up and Roxie put the phone down.

So much was at stake, making the wrong decision now could prove fatal. It was best to do as Aunt Katie said and try to find a balance. Find a way to fix the unfixable, basically. But how?

10

Roxie

The next morning found Roxie holding a hand to her chest, trying to remember how to breathe. She'd just received a text notification from June and she was afraid to open it. Sitting at the little table on the balcony, a coffee cup full beside her, Roxie wondered if this was more trouble coming her way or if her one-time BFF was about to prove she was still just that.

Roxie inhaled a shaky breath and flicked the lock screen away to tap on the message. She really wished she had some peach gummies right about now. She could use something to gnaw on to ease her tension. Moving her eyes up to the screen, Roxie looked at the text and felt…relief.

Hey, I'm leaving town tomorrow and wanted to spend some time with you. Where are you?

The text was simple enough, there was no 'you broke my brother's heart, how could you, I'm going to break your face' or anything else along those lines. Just a simple request to see Roxie before June had to leave.

Roxie typed in the address, afraid to say anything more. She'd been on the verge of tears since she woke up, her nerves too fractured and frayed to remain calm. The sound of seagulls as they swooped through the sky had made her burst into tears when she first settled into the wicker chair earlier. Now, actually typing words seemed to renew the threat of that happening again.

There'd just been too much thrown at her lately and even the slightest hint of more stress had her on the verge of chewing her nails down to nubs. Which was something, because she'd never chewed her nails before. But stress can make a person batshit crazy, couldn't it? She thought, staring down at the phone screen.

A new message popped up and Roxie breathed a huge sigh of relief.

Be there in 10. Bringing tacos, get out the napkins.

Roxie's relief nearly dropped her to the floor, but she managed to stay upright. Knowing that June was likely serious about the tacos had her up on her feet in the next breath, picking out plates and glasses to put on the table outside. There was also an entire package of napkins, so Roxie took that out to the balcony.

She waited in the kitchen, almost putting some music on, but changed her mind. June would obviously want to talk and would have a thousand questions; music would just be a distraction. A quick run to the bathroom revealed her hair was still in the messy bun she'd put it in earlier, her white t-shirt was clean, as were the denim shorts that skimmed her upper thighs with ragged tendrils of cloth. She looked like she was twelve years old without a speck of makeup on, but it was June, she didn't need to look like a cover model, did she?

A discreet knock on the door had her rushing back to the kitchen to open it.

"Hey, girl! Nice place!" June's bright smile put any last worries Roxie had to rest.

"It's my friend Nick's place." Roxie brushed off the compliment and closed the door once June was inside.

"And who is Nick? Should I be mad at you?" June's beautifully outlined eyes smiled with affection tinged with a slight hint of menace.

Roxie stared at Lincoln's sister realizing she might have made a mistake. "Um, he's really just a friend, June. And last I heard; Lincoln didn't want me anywhere near him anyway." Roxie spoke carefully, but with the determination she'd learned to face the world with a long time ago.

"Calm down, calm down. I was only teasing." June held up two plastic bags filled with food and drinks. "Taco truce?"

"Taco truce." Roxie smiled, happy the moment was over with. She knew there'd probably be more to come, but so far so good.

They were down six tacos each by the time Roxie sat back, calling time on the taco extravaganza. "I can't eat anymore, even if they are tiny."

"They're good, aren't they? It was some little place that the online reviews said I shouldn't miss. And I have to admit, I thought you might not be able to say no to tacos." June wiped her mouth with a napkin, the gimlet shine of mischief in her eyes now replaced with sadness. "Lincoln told me about Lily."

"I thought he might have." Roxie picked up her glass of iced tea and stared at it before she spoke again. "I guess you're mad at me too?"

"Not at all, Roxie. You were a child, a traumatized child. Okay, so we thought we were grown at eighteen and nineteen, but we weren't, were we? You made the choice you thought was best for everyone." The sad eyes were filled with understanding now. "And I know Lincoln; you probably tried to tell him and he just barged through whatever you tried to say."

"Yes, he did." Roxie's words trailed off, her brain suddenly empty. She struggled to get her train of thought back, grabbed one more taco, and unwrapped the paper from around it. "I should have told him though. Finding out from Nathan must have been heartbreaking."

"I know we haven't really talked a lot about what happened, but if you changed your name and moved this far away, you must have been terrified. And not taking the baby with you was smart too. Those men might be looking for you and if they found you with your daughter, who knows what might have happened?" June's head tilted as if to say, 'what can you do'? "It must have been a really hard decision for you. She's the only family you have left."

"How do you always see the good in the crazy decisions I make?" Roxie asked, the tears threatening again. "I think I could murder a stranger and you'd find a reason why they deserved it."

"You're probably right, but I know you, Roxie. I've known you since you were Chloe, and I know your heart." June reached for her hand, something they always seemed to do with each other. Their friendship wasn't just about talking and listening, it was about human contact and affection that made them more sisters than friends. That had always been the case, time and distance hadn't changed that. "You aren't a bad person and you aren't evil, Rox. You always want what's best for others. You think of yourself last, even when you should be thinking of yourself first. That's why."

"You make me sound like an angel and I promise you that I'm not." Roxie clenched June's hand in return, but she shook her head just the same. "I'm not perfect."

"No, you aren't. But you try to be good. That's what matters. I grew up, we both grew up, with privileged families as our role models. We knew what snobbery was and when racism reared its ugly head at school and people made fun of my eyes or how short I was, you never backed down. I still remember you punching Stephanie Meadows in the nose when she called me that nasty name." June's eyes became distant and she laughed quietly before her gaze came back to Roxie. "Whatever you chose to do, it was the right decision. Don't let Lincoln make you think any different."

"I hope he'll calm down at some point and not be so angry with me." Roxie picked the tea up and gulped what was left. "I can't keep crying like some lovelorn teenager."

"Do you want to patch things up with him?" June asked softly, her lips pursed as if she wished she could draw the words back.

"I would like to, but I don't see how he'll ever forgive me." Roxie shook herself and focused on June. "I'm tired of talking about him, tell me more about your life now."

"I'm still an overworked doctor in New York. It's the same as it always was, overcrowded, full of people always on the move, and demanding what they want with rude voices." June sighed this time, her hand on her forehead for a moment. "But Liam's just as overworked as I am. He's the head of cardiology at Dad's hospital. Dad's setting him up to take over that department in the hospital. I'll have the infertility treatment center to deal with. It's a lot of work for both of us."

Roxie smiled at the mention of Liam, but she didn't push for information. That crush was a dream she'd left behind a long time ago. She still had the last note he'd left in the birdhouse for her, but it had never been a serious relationship. Even if the letters contained some of the sweetest words she'd ever read. "I'm glad Liam's doing well in his career."

"He is, and Dad wants him to hurry up and take over so that he can retire. Dad has a new girlfriend and they want to travel the world together." June rolled her eyes with a smile. "At least this one is of sensible age. I'm tired of him dating young women my age."

"Seriously? His girlfriends were that young?" Roxie sat forward, her curiosity piqued.

"Mmhmm, I think some of them were younger than me, but you know what? He deserves to have some fun after putting up with Mom's bullshit for so long," June answered and started to clear up the garbage around them. "I love Mom, don't get me wrong, but she's a bit schizo sometimes."

"I remember." Roxie nodded, aware of just how unpredictable Ms. Young could be. "I'm glad he's finding happiness now."

"I am too, really." June got up and took the trash into the house. "I'll take that out when I leave."

"Thanks. I'm trying not to go out too much. Not because I'm afraid or anything, but because I'm just trying to lie low." Roxie frowned, wondering if she'd contradicted herself. "Anyway, thanks for everything."

"So what happened with you and Lincoln in the beginning?" June waylaid her with that unexpected question once they'd sat down on the couch in the living room. "I mean, you hated him."

"I did, I thought. Until that night." Roxie's words trailed off, remembering her fear, her need to be comforted. "I think it was the trauma that made it happen. He didn't say no, I didn't say no, it just happened."

"I can understand that." June nodded but waited for more.

"Then I found out I was pregnant. I could only remember one phone number, Aunt Katie's. By the time I found out I was pregnant I had three jobs and lived over the pizza restaurant that was one of the places I worked at. I knew I couldn't take care of a baby or raise one there. Aunt Katie took me in, helped me until Lily was a few months old, and we talked about it. I decided I'd leave them and go find better work, far away, to keep them both safe." Roxie stopped suddenly, the pain of leaving her baby behind too overwhelming to ignore for a moment. "It nearly killed me. I nearly turned around and went back thousands of times. She has the same face as you and Lincoln, but my eyes. It's like looking at all three of us at one time. And she was so sweet, loved me so completely."

Roxie's mouth closed on a sob, her eyes dripped with tears, and she stared at nothing, the pain still raw and inescapable. June came over to kneel down in front of Roxie so she could hug her. "I miss her so much, June."

"I'm sure you do, honey," June soothed, rubbing her hand up and down Roxie's back.

Roxie couldn't stop the sobs for a moment, even when she realized some of that pain was from Lincoln, and not being with him. From how angry he'd been with her for trying to protect her daughter from all threats. He could be mad all he wanted to be; he hadn't been there. Yeah, that was her fault, but still.

"You know, honey, Lincoln still doesn't know who his father is. Or if he's even alive still. Mom won't tell him who his real father is. I think that's what he's really angry about, that you've done to Lily what Mom has done to him. And he's always wanted children. There's a lot of unspoken pain behind his anger," June revealed to Roxie, once Roxie's sobs calmed a little. "I think if you approach him with that knowledge, understand that about him, then it'll be easier to understand why he's so mad."

"Holy fucking moly, you're right." Roxie blinked and pulled away, so much is making sense now. Some of it she'd kind of known, or had known once upon a time, but it hadn't all come together in her mind the way June had just laid it out. "I did the exact same thing, didn't I? Fuck."

Roxie thought about a few things and then spoke again. "That's why he's taking care of all of those people in Cambodia, isn't it? He wants to help people, to take care of children, to help families stay together. And what did I do? I tore away his only child."

"Don't take on all the blame there, Roxie. It's hurt him, yes, but Mom has a lot to answer for as well." June paused, looked at Roxie steadily, and came to a decision. "Can we see her?"

"Lily? When it's safe to, yes." Roxie nodded but frowned. "When I can be sure that Lincoln isn't going to snatch her away from me."

"I don't think that's going to happen right away,"

June said, openly and honestly. "He has to prove he has a right to first."

"He does, yeah."

"He has always had a crush on you. I didn't realize that until the last couple of days." June grinned, her right hand in her hair, her elbow braced on the back of the couch. "I started thinking about when we were kids and Lincoln was always *there*. I know you had a crush on Liam, but it was Lincoln that had the crush on you. It didn't make sense back then, why he was always around because all he did was pick on us, but he'd always find an excuse to be the one to pick me up from your house. He'd bring Liam along, but now I can see, he just wanted to see you."

"Oh, I don't know about that." Roxie grinned, but her cheeks turned pink.

"He tried so hard to find you after you disappeared, too." June paused, her lips twisting in thought. "He found out a lot, but that's for him to tell."

"What do you mean?" Roxie asked, confused. He'd found out a lot about what?

"It's stuff Lincoln will have to explain, he's the one who knows all the details. Anyway, I think it's time for me to go. I have to pack still and get ready to leave tomorrow. I hate to say goodbye, but I won't be gone for long this time. I promise."

"I hope not." Roxie stood up to hug her friend, June's

words still bouncing around in her head. What had that all meant? "Let me know when you get home. Love you."

"Love you too, Roxie. Always," June hugged her and gave her a quick cheek peck before she grabbed her bag and the trash and left.

What exactly had she meant, Roxie wondered, staring at the door.

11

Lincoln

June was going back to New York and Lincoln would be alone. He didn't have Roxie to fill his nights anymore, he'd made sure of that, for better or worse.

At the moment, it seemed like the right decision to have made, but it felt like the worst decision he'd ever made. She'd kept something vitally important from him, he couldn't trust her now, could he? He remembered that vulnerable, virginal girl he'd made love to all those years ago, because that's how it had been.

He'd adored her for many years and that night had been a dream come true for him. It had been her worst nightmare, but for him, what they'd shared had been beautiful. Born from trauma yes, but still beautiful. He'd hoped that things would change, that she'd let him protect her, but she'd been gone when he came back from getting breakfast.

It was clear she was afraid, not of him, but of what had happened to her parents. That must have colored every decision she'd made since then. But he could have taken care of her. His mom and Dr. Bennet would have helped them both, he could have been a dad and, maybe, a husband.

He wouldn't have forced her to marry him, but he'd have asked. He'd have done whatever was necessary to protect her and his child. His child. Every time he thought those words, he got chills. There was a small soul out there that was his.

A buzz of his phone and he saw he had a text message from Tanya, one of his PAs.

Monica says she's at this address. The address followed. *It belongs to that guy Nick she's been seen with before.*

"Well, fuck." Lincoln said out loud, pissed at himself. He'd driven her to run to that guy again.

Lincoln couldn't help but roll his eyes at his own stupidity. Of course, she'd hide in one of that guy's places. Where else would she go?

From Monica's previous reports, this Nick guy owned a lot of property, had enough money to run his own kingdom for generations to come, and was more than capable of providing security that could keep even

Lincoln from getting anywhere near Roxie. Which was probably for the best, for now.

He needed time to think, alone. He needed to get his head around all of this. Alone. Picking up a six-pack of beer from the fridge, Lincoln walked out to the beach, headed for the sun lounger with his light blue bathrobe flowing around his legs. He didn't give a fuck if anyone saw him in his boxer shorts and robe. He needed to think, and this was where he did it best. Cracking open the first bottle top of many, Lincoln settled in to watch the ocean until it gave him an answer.

A week passed before he finally made a decision. He needed to talk to Roxie. He wasn't angry anymore; he was just resolved to do what was right. He thought about shaving but decided not to. Fuck it. A shower was enough. And clean clothes, of course.

He sent her a text message, asking to meet up with her.

She answered back after a half-hour, with an address to a café near the condo. Good. She was willing to talk to him at least. He drove to the place, parked, and went to find a table. Roxie was already seated, dressed in a blue maxi dress with a denim jacket on over it.

She looked as beautiful as always, but her eyes were hidden behind aviator sunglasses, despite the overcast sky. She was still hiding from him then.

Lincoln wore a pair of dark blue slacks, a white

button-up top, but the blazer that went with the suit was snagged over his shoulder by a finger. He kept his sunglasses on too. "Thanks for agreeing to see me."

"It's the least I could do," she responded, not getting up to greet him. But then, why would she, he reminded himself.

"How are you doing?" He asked once a waiter came and took his order for a cappuccino.

"I'm fine, Lincoln. What are we doing here?" She asked, her leg bouncing with unhidden impatience.

"I thought we should talk." He paused, noting how she sat back, further away from him. That stung, but he shouldn't expect anything less.

"About what? About how you plan to take my daughter from me for good?" Her eyebrows peeked out from the top of her shades, making her point. She was pissed and that was one big clue.

"No. Yes. Fuck, Rox, please? Let me explain." He went quiet as the waiter brought his coffee, waiting until the man was gone before he spoke again. "Tell me about her, please?"

"She loves ballet, like her mommy. And piano like her dad," Roxie said blankly, but then her lips twitched. "She's always putting on plays she's written and loves talking to me on video calls. I see her at Christmas, her birthday, and when I can during the school holidays. I don't get back to New York often enough to see her, but that's for her own good."

"So she won't get too close to you?" Lincoln asked, a little snottier than he planned to.

Her frown made him wince.

"So I won't expose her to anything bad that might follow behind me, you asshole," Roxie hissed once she'd leaned forward, the angry purse of her lips probably not as deadly as her eyes were. It was good she still had those sunglasses on.

"Sorry, I deserved that."

"You did. Oh, she plays the violin as well," Roxie mentioned, leaning back, not quite relaxed but not on the verge of clawing his eyes out now. "Really well. She plays so beautifully it brings tears to my eyes."

"I want to get to know her," he said hesitantly, not wanting to set her off again, but he wanted to make his intentions clear. "She deserves to know who her father is."

Roxie didn't say anything for a long time. "If you take her, make me one promise, Lincoln? As her mother, as someone you used to care about, please do one thing for me?"

"What's that?" He said, not committing to anything just now.

"That you'll take Aunt Katie with her. She knows Aunt

Katie, loves her, and Katie adores Lily. Separating them might be even worse than taking me from her permanently. She'd hate you forever if you took Katie from her too. I promise you that." Roxie's words shook a little but steadied as she carried on. "If you want to form any kind of bond with her, uprooting her and taking away everything she knows and loves will make sure you do the opposite."

"I see your point," Lincoln conceded, nodding his head. "I agree."

"Good."

"But I do know what it's like to grow up without a father. Lily doesn't have to endure that. I can keep that pain from her life," he offered, still not sure about what he was going to do exactly. He did know he wanted his daughter with him, where he'd know she was safe. Maybe what Roxie suggested was the best way to turn the situation into a good thing, instead of a trauma for Lily.

Because yeah, he was an asshole, but he didn't want to traumatize his daughter. He wanted to protect her from all the things that caused her pain. He wanted custody of her, but he wouldn't keep Roxie from seeing her. That's what he'd decided after a week of staring into the ocean for an answer that never came.

He'd have to take Lily, but he'd also have to allow her to see her mother. That was the only way to keep from breaking the girl's heart. He just wasn't sure when to tell Roxie that.

At the moment, he had no plans of starting their relationship again, even if his head told him to call her at every waking moment of his day, and even in his dreams. Trust had been broken, and that would take some time to heal. If it ever did heal.

"I know you didn't know your dad, but you did know your mom, Lincoln. And whether it was a wise decision or not, she did what she thought was best for you," Roxie started but he interrupted with a wave.

"What my mother did has no bearing on the here and now, Roxie. You decided to keep my daughter from me. Okay, you say you did it to protect us both, but I can't accept that right now. I'm trying to be fair here, I'm trying to do what's best for Lily, but don't make this harder than it has to be." He watched her face but there wasn't so much as a twitch, just a nod of acceptance.

"Fine. I can understand that." She inhaled, drawing her nostrils in a little as she did so and he almost smiled. That had always been one of the cutest things he'd never told her about. How much he loved everything about her, even the way her nostrils drew in when she inhaled through her nose.

"How are you otherwise?" He asked, wondering if she'd tell him about staying at Nick's place or not. It wasn't a test, just curiosity.

"I'm fine," she said, back to the closed-off Roxie he'd met all those months ago. "How are you?"

"I'm good," he said, despite the beard he'd grown because he couldn't be bothered to shave. He thought it suited him, but it itched like fuck, so he'd probably shave it off sooner or later.

"Good. Anything else?" All business now, she was ready to go and not above hiding just how ready she was to get away.

"Just this, please don't break off all contact with me. I do plan on getting custody of Lily, but if we can keep this civil, I'd like to. You can still have visitation with her," he said, but she just smirked at him.

"How generous of you," she drawled out in a perfect example of the accent she'd picked up in her years in South Carolina.

It suited her.

"I'm sorry, Roxie. I think it's best for her." He held his hands out with a shrug. "Can you tell me I'm wrong?"

She watched him silently, her lips twisted, before she shook her head. "You're probably right. I've been able to take care of her from afar all this time, but you can give her a lot more than I can. And I can see her when I want to?"

"Yes, of course. I'll bring her down here if you like?"

"I'll talk to Aunt Katie, see what she thinks. She's got to have some input into this too." Roxie shifted around in her seat, restless but trying to remain calm. "I'll call you later, shall I?"

"That's fine." Lincoln couldn't keep the relief out of his voice. "I'll keep her safe, Roxie. I promise."

"You'd better, Lincoln, or I will make you wish you'd never set eyes on me." Roxie's grim voice made that promise far more than a deadly warning. "She may not live with me, but she is my daughter. I love her more than anything else in this world. I wouldn't allow this at all if I didn't think you could protect her, but I promise you, if you fail, if you fuck this up and she ends up hating you, I will get her back, one way or another."

"Even with those men out there, Roxie?" He reminded, wanting to wound her for her doubt in him as a caring parent.

"Even with those men out there, Lincoln." She pulled her glasses down as she repeated the words back to him. "I will make you disappear if you hurt her in any way."

"I believe you," he said after a long pause. She had the right. She was Lily's mother, after all.

"Good. Are we done now?" Roxie asked, and Lincoln nodded at her untouched mocha. "I don't want it and I have another appointment. Are we done?"

"Yes, I guess we are." Lincoln pulled his lips in for a moment, to stop the words that would beg her to come back to his place. "If you need anything, Roxie, let me know."

"Yeah, sure, Lincoln," she said and picked up her bag. "Take care."

She left then, her back straight, without another word.

It was plain to him that she was still hurt, and he couldn't blame her, he'd been vicious to her. Now that he'd had time to calm down, time to think about what she'd said, he knew she'd been right. She'd tried to tell him, but he'd talked over her, ignored the need in her eyes, at a point when he was vulnerable himself.

It must have been hard to get the courage up to tell him something like that after so many years. He still didn't like that she hadn't told him from the moment she found out she was pregnant, but now he could see how a teenager had made a decision that would prove to be a bombshell later.

But if they couldn't go back to being lovers, he would like to be her friend. They shared a child, whether she liked it or not. He wanted them to be civil to each other. Maybe she just needed her own time to process all of this.

Because what June had said did hit home. Since she was eighteen, Roxie had bounced from one trauma to the next, holding herself above water somehow, but never seeming to catch a break. If he could make this latest event less traumatic, he would. He still cared deeply about her. He couldn't deny that one bit.

Now he just had to find a way to convince her that he wasn't going to screw her over completely, because that was something else he'd come to realize about her. Men had screwed her over in one way or another since she was eighteen. He refused to be one more in a long list of assholes. Even if she thought he was the biggest asshole of all.

12

Lincoln

$\mathcal{L}$incoln looked at his watch while his foot tapped on the black marble floor of the restaurant. He'd asked Roxie to meet him for dinner when she called him after their meeting at the café. She'd talked to Aunt Katie and had agreed to dinner to discuss the outcome.

He was seated in a secluded section, per his request, but he could see the entrance and knew the moment she walked in. She was dressed in a black wraparound dress with black leather boots. Her hair, still black and purple, was curled around her shoulders in delicate waves. All in all, she was as beautiful, as tempting, as ever, but she wasn't his anymore.

For a moment he wasn't sure if it was the pain of loss or her beauty that stole his breath away. Never one to let his emotions run away with him, Lincoln got his mind and body back under control and stood up as the waiter brought her to the table to be seated.

"Good evening," Roxie said and sat down across from him, her eyes barely touching on his before they moved away.

Her blue eyes were incredible, as always, but they would not meet his. She didn't want to be here, that was obvious, but she'd come anyway. She always had been brave.

"Good evening, Roxie. How are you?" He answered once the waiter took her order for a glass of sparkling water.

"I'm fine, Lincoln." Her eyes came up to his now, half defiant, half…defeated? No, that wasn't the right word, he decided. Resigned perhaps, but not defeated. "I spoke with Aunt Katie. She and Lily will be on a flight tonight. She'd like to introduce Lily to you, before we go any further. Lily has a life in New York, after all, friends at school and lessons that she may not want to give up. I think we should allow her to decide whether she wants to live down here with you or stay in New York. In which case, you'd have to go back to New York permanently. There wouldn't be much point in taking her from her life if you planned on staying down here while she's up there. Would there?"

"I see your point, yes," he conceded and clasped his hands together on the table between them. "If she wants to stay in New York does that mean you'd be moving back?"

"No, it doesn't. I don't have a life there anymore and I don't think I'd have an easy time making contacts there. It took me years to build up the following that I have now, an older face on a fresh scene isn't going to get much attention in my line of work." She frowned at him, looked away, and put her hands together in her lap. "I would like to be near Lily, but I don't think I'd ever be able to call New York home again after my parents' deaths."

"I understand." It was an awkward conversation for two people who had been emotionally connected only a few weeks ago. He hated that things had turned out like this, but this was the situation they found themselves in. "Would you like to look at the menu?"

"Yeah, sure. Their plane won't land until after 9 pm, so there's time to kill." Roxie picked up the black menu and started to read.

Lincoln watched her for a moment, pondering what to say or ask. There was only one real question he had. "Does she know she's coming to meet me?"

"Not yet, I'll explain it later when I go to pick her up." Roxie's face was so tight it looked like it might shatter if she moved any muscle around her mouth too much. "Let me have her for one more night? Please?"

"Sure, of course." Lincoln wouldn't have been so agreeable a few days ago, but now that he'd calmed down a little, he could be a little forgiving. "But I would like to meet her tomorrow."

"Come by my place around lunchtime then. I'll have had time to explain things to her by then." Roxie put the menu down and brought her eyes up to his. "I owe her an explanation as much as I owed you one."

"Alright." Lincoln nodded, seeing her point. Even if he really hadn't wanted to hear her explanation at the time, she had given him one. Lily deserved that too. "Just text me when you're ready then."

"I will." She didn't look pleased to be here, but who could blame her for that? She was in a position she couldn't get out of.

They ate their dinner in silence, a dinner where Lincoln kept thinking about how he'd meet his daughter properly the next day. He finished eating, wiped his mouth with a napkin, and pushed his plate away. "You know, I always wanted to know who my father was."

"I can imagine so," Roxie replied, a slight frown marring her forehead.

"I used to ask my mom who he was, but she'd never tell me. My first stepfather definitely wasn't my dad, he barely even acknowledged I existed. I called him Daddy a few times and he got so angry about it, shouted at me to tell me he wasn't my father and I wasn't to call him that. Every time my mother picked up a new man, I wondered if he was really my father and she'd gotten back together with him. And then she married June's dad, and I couldn't have had a better father. I wanted very much for him to be my dad. He tried at least, even if he wasn't my real father." Lincoln's words tapered off, lost in thought. Roxie remained quiet and Lincoln finally picked up where he'd left off. "I think Mom thought that as long as I had a male role model, it didn't matter if they were my blood relative or not. She didn't get that I wanted to know that man, to see what my future might be, to... I don't know, have a bond with him. She would brush off my questions and tell me that I didn't need to know him."

Lincoln's words became heated as he continued to speak, the words and anger unacknowledged and unspoken for so long pouring out of him. "You can't do the same thing to Lily, Roxie. You don't understand how incomplete she'll feel."

Roxie, quiet until then, spoke up. Lincoln frowned, wondering what had brought the fire to her eyes and the blood to her cheeks. She leaned forward and spoke with a quiet hiss. "I think I know just how incomplete a person can feel without their parents, Lincoln."

He had the good grace to look away then and felt shame as a sharp sting in his neck. Of course, she was right, she'd lost both of her parents. He wanted to point out that she'd known them, even for a short time, but that would be crass and cruel.

"Is there a problem?" A male voice asked. Lincoln looked up and immediately saw red.

Nick. Just great, the man that wanted Roxie for himself was here, barging in on their conversation. "No, there wasn't until just now, actually."

Nick's eyes narrowed at Lincoln's words, but he turned his back on Lincoln to face Roxie. "Shall I take you home, Roxie?"

"Yes please," she said softly as she stood up. "Lincoln, I'll message you tomorrow. Thank you for dinner."

Lincoln watched as Roxie left with Nick, the guy she seemed to prefer to be with right now. He swallowed down the angry words he wanted to say, clenched his fist by his side, and let them go. Once he'd calmed down, he signaled the waiter and asked for the bill. It was time to go home, alone again.

It was only when he was sitting in the kitchen, looking out at the ocean later, that he realized just how thoughtless he'd been. He'd been trying to explain to Roxie what it would be like for Lily to grow up without him, all the while, she'd had to grow up very quickly because her parents had been murdered.

Which brought up the matter of how he'd still not told her about that, or the evidence he'd managed to get together since she disappeared. June told him that he needed to tell Roxie about the whole situation, but he forgot about it every time he saw her. Even tonight, he'd wanted to bring her back to the house and strip her out of that beautiful, but way too concealing dress.

And the secret room there, where she'd shown him a variety of ways to give pleasure through pain, exquisitely beautiful moments that he wouldn't have erased from his memory for any amount of money. Then he found himself in the studio he'd had done up for her. There'd been a plan forming in his mind when he had this room created. A future that he hadn't quite named yet, but a future, nevertheless.

The news about Lily had done a number on him, and now he'd destroyed whatever future there might have been between them. Now there would be the kind of tense dinners they'd had that evening, and Roxie going home with another man.

Lincoln was certain Roxie wasn't sleeping with the guy, but what if she was? He had no right to her anymore, he'd made that clear the night she left the house for good. He'd all but driven her into that guy's arms. At least he was a decent man, he'd learned that much when he had Nick investigated. Lincoln hated Nick because he was a threat to what he'd had with Roxie, and as long as that guy was around, there'd probably be no hope of rebuilding his relationship with her.

The guy was way too protective of Roxie, as she deserved, to let Lincoln get anywhere near her. Which was probably for the best, at this point. He couldn't ask her to come back to him, not after the way he'd treated her. His anger had burned hot, but it had burned out fast. With Nick in the way, there was no way to get Roxie back.

For now, he'd focus on Lily, making sure she was happy and could settle into a life with him as her father. Who knew, the girl might hate him for taking her away from her life, for intruding on it. Just because he'd longed to know his real father didn't mean she did, did it? Doubts began to eat at him, and for the first time, Lincoln wondered if he'd made a mistake.

Would Lily hate him if he made her come live with him? He was her father, yes, but he was a stranger. Would it matter to her when he was just a strange man who took her from her life?

Doubts ate at him, and he ended up leaving the studio his daughter could now use, to go sit outside on the deck at the back of the house. He'd have to empty out the playroom, there was nobody else he'd want to take in there but Roxie and he knew she wouldn't be coming back to him for a while, if at all. For now, he'd leave the room. There were too many memories in there, too many emotions he needed to put away.

He was a father, something he'd always wanted, so now he'd have to think like a father, act like a father, and put the hopes and plans he'd had for the girl's mother to the side. He wanted to call Roxie, ask her what colors Lily's favorites were so that he could have a room prepared for her. He knew she liked playing piano and the violin, that she was in love with ballet as much as her mother had been at the same age, but what else should he know about her?

Roxie knew all of these things, she could reveal all the things Lincoln should know, but calling her right now would be a bad idea. The look on her face as she left the table was a mix of hurt and bitter anger. Lincoln couldn't blame her for that, he'd stepped his foot in it, big time.

He checked his watch and walked back into the house. It was after 9 pm, Lily's plane should arrive any minute. He wanted to go and see her now, to demand Roxie let him come to her place tonight, but she had to explain the situation to Lily. Would it be easy for her, he wondered, or would Lily be upset with her mother?

Lincoln hoped his daughter would be excited to meet

him, that she'd want to find out who he was as much as he'd wanted to know who his own father was. That missing link still gnawed at him sometimes. It was doubtful that his mother would ever tell him the identity of the man who'd created him, and that left a hole in Lincoln's life. He didn't want that for Lily, so while this may all take some getting used to, some time to adjust to, he wanted his daughter to have what he would never have. If he had to walk through broken glass to do it, he'd make sure she grew up knowing that he wanted to be a part of her life and that he'd always be there for her.

Lincoln's phone buzzed and he picked it up, hoping that Roxie had changed her mind and wanted him to come tonight. That wasn't the case though, it was just some company that wanted to talk to him about his car's extended warranty, and Lincoln had to clamp down on the urge to throw his phone.

The tedium of life brought reality home to him though. At some point in the future, he'd know all of this stuff about his daughter, he'd be used to having her with him, and all his worries about whether she'd like him or not would be in the past. Their life might become as mundane as that stupid email he'd just got on his phone.

Would he ever really take having Lily with him for granted though? That would be awful, and he doubted that he'd ever do that. Only time would tell.

Instead of spending the rest of the night mooning over what might or might not be, Lincoln went into his office and opened up his laptop. He'd get some work done and then head to bed. Maybe he'd sleep late, so he wouldn't pace all the next morning, waiting to hear from Roxie. One could hope, anyway.

13

Roxie

"**M**ommy, why are we here?" Lily's girlish voice asked as Roxie drove them back from the airport.

"Well, I know I usually come up to see you, but there's someone you have to meet tomorrow. A person that is very…important to you," Roxie answered, not wanting to get into the conversation right now but Lily had the sense to know that being there with her mother meant something was different.

She was a smart cookie, Roxie thought with pride.

"Okay," Lily answered, and went back to staring out of her window in the backseat of Roxie's car.

"How are you, honey?" Aunt Katie asked, and Roxie glanced over at her with a faint smile.

"I'm handling it all, I guess," Roxie spoke softly, not wanting Lily to hear too much. "I told him he could come over at lunchtime tomorrow."

"Okay. Is he still as handsome as he was when he was a boy?" Aunt Katie asked with a charming smile on her lined face. She'd aged in the ten years since the fire, they all had, but she wore it well.

Katie's hair was long, but she always kept it pinned up in a neat bun, and her clothes were always clean and elegant. They might not outshine high society labels, but they were good quality and serviceable. It was Katie's complexion that had always fascinated Roxie though. Even with the lines of age creeping across her face, it was unblemished and peachy in color.

"He is as handsome as he always was, Aunt Katie," Roxie finally answered, knowing she couldn't stall the questions the older woman would have.

"I suppose he's anxious to meet her?" Aunt Katie asked quietly, her eyes darting back to Lily before coming back to the front of the car.

"He is, I keep expecting to get a message demanding I bring her over to him tonight, but I think he's calmed down a little. For now. Who knows what tomorrow will bring? It's Lincoln, after all. He's not used to being made to wait."

"He's waited this long, a few more hours won't kill him," Aunt Katie sniped, but her anger wasn't directed at

Roxie. That was totally reserved for Lincoln. "He might be handsome, and smart, and rich, but this is really so stupid of him."

"It's okay, really." Roxie took one hand off the steering wheel to pat Katie's left hand. "Now that he's calmed down, what he says makes sense. He has things I can't provide for her. And he should get to know her anyway."

"I know you're right, but I just feel so angry about it all." Aunt Katie moved around in her seat, adjusting herself until she found a more comfortable position. "I just, oh I don't know what I want to do, but I want to do something."

"You can do something, make this as easy for Lily as you possibly can. I know you love her deeply, and even if this takes a turn for the worse, if I know you're with her, I know she'll be okay." Roxie glanced back at Lily, but the little girl had headphones in her ears now, her lips moving silently along to whatever song she had on.

"She will be, you know I'll protect her with my life." Aunt Katie sighed deeply and looked out of the window on her side again. "It is nice here. Is it warmer in the winters than back home? I've heard coastal towns can be cold in the wintertime."

"It's not so bad, really. Sometimes it can be down-right chilly, but it's tolerable most days." Roxie shrugged and flicked the indicator switch up to turn into the parking garage. "The summers are amazing, but the influx of tourists can make it a nightmare. Otherwise, I think you'll like it here. It's not Florida, but it's not that bad."

"I'll have to give it a try, I guess." Aunt Katie opened her door once Roxie pulled to a stop and turned the engine off. "Let me help with our bags."

"I can manage, just wait with Lily for a second." Roxie soon had the bags out and they were all going up to her apartment in the elevator. "I'll sleep on the couch while you two are here. Lily can have the small bedroom and you can have the larger one, Aunt Katie."

"Oh honey, I don't want to put you out," Aunt Katie said with a frown, but Roxie just shook her head.

"I'm not making you sleep on that couch, no matter how comfortable I think it might be. Your back won't tolerate sleeping on that thing for long." Roxie opened the door to the apartment and brought in her guests. "It's only a small place, but it'll do for now."

"Wow, Mommy! Is that the ocean?" Lily ran to stare out of the sliding glass doors at the ocean beyond. "Can I go out there?"

"In a minute, honey, let's put your stuff away first, okay?" Roxie called and Lily came rushing back to help.

"Can I go swimming tomorrow?" Lily asked as Roxie opened up the first suitcase filled with her daughter's clothes. They were good quality and all in good shape.

Aunt Katie didn't waste the money Roxie sent her and she knew it.

"I don't know, baby. It's been kind of cold lately, and you have to meet someone tomorrow." Roxie looked over her shoulder as she hung the clothes on hangers to see Lily staring at her solemnly.

"Who is this person I have to meet, Mommy?" Lily's eyes looking, her mouth set in an unhappy line. Roxie had seen that same look on Lincoln's face a dozen times and on June's even more often.

It nearly broke Roxie's heart looking at how upset her daughter was and that made the decision for her. She'd tell Lily tonight about her father. There was no good to be had in making Lily wait.

"Well, you're going to meet your father tomorrow, Lily," Roxie replied as she came to sit beside her on the narrow bed.

"Oh," Lily said very quietly, her brows furrowing deeper together, until even her forehead was wrinkled up a little. "I have a father?"

"Well, yes, honey, of course you have a father. Do you want to see him?" Roxie pulled her phone out of her back pocket, grateful that she'd come home to change before she'd gone to pick up her rather untraditional little family. Wearing jeans meant she could keep her phone on her all the time. "This is him."

Roxie scrolled through her pictures until she found

one from their time in Cambodia, Lincoln was smiling a carefree smile and laughter lit up his entire face. Then she scrolled some more and found a picture of him on the beach, sitting in the sun lounger, just enjoying the warmth and the sunshine. "This is him."

Lily held the phone, her hands over her mother's, as she stared at the man she hadn't known existed. But that was because Roxie had never told her who he was. Of course, Lily had never asked, but she must have wondered.

"He's very handsome," Lily said, a small finger coming out to touch somewhere around Lincoln's face. "Do I look like him?"

"You do, and your Aunt June too, his sister. She was my best friend all my life until I turned eighteen. We lost touch for a while, but she's in my life again. You'll meet her soon too. I'm not sure when, but you will."

Aunt Katie came to the door and Roxie looked up, lost and unsure of how to tell Lily the next part. Aunt Katie's lips pursed in a 'be strong' kind of way and she nodded at Roxie. After a deep breath, Roxie continued. "If you want to, you can come down here and live with him. Or you can stay in New York and live with him there."

"But I live with Aunt Katie, Mommy. I can't live with my daddy." Lily shook her head and gave Roxie a look that questioned whether her mommy was silly or not.

"Well, soon you're going to have to go live with him. Aunt Katie will be coming with you, I promise." Roxie rushed to add in that last bit. "And if you come down here, maybe I can see you every day?"

"Oh, that would be wonderful," Lily spoke with excitement now and happiness shining in her eyes. "I miss you when you're gone, Mommy."

"And I miss you, baby. I really do." Roxie pulled Lily close and blinked away tears she didn't want to shed. Tears might upset Lily, and Roxie wanted to avoid that at all costs.

"So, if I like my daddy, I'm going to stay with him? What if I don't?" Lily pulled back from her mother to ask.

Roxie's eyes shot up to Aunt Katie's and begged for an answer to give her daughter. Aunt Katie shrugged, as lost as Roxie was on that one. "Well, honey, I think you're going to love your dad and you won't have to worry about that at all. You'll see, he's a great guy and he's so looking forward to meeting you."

"I don't know, Mommy." Lily turned around on the edge of the bed and looked down at her feet. "What if he doesn't like me?"

"What do you mean, what if he doesn't like you? Why wouldn't he like you, baby?" Roxie brushed blonde hair from her daughter's face, a face that was the perfect blend of her father and mother's best features, a beautiful, trusting face, that just wanted reassurance.

"Because I'm not into sports, or I don't know, maybe he doesn't like kids and that's why he wasn't around before?" Lily shrugged as if it didn't matter, but the way her shoulders stooped spelled it all out for Roxie. Lily was worried she wasn't good enough.

"Listen, your dad wasn't around because, well, I thought it would be better if it was just you and me and Aunt Katie. He knows about you now, though, and he wants to be in your life. He's going to adore you, Lily, and I think you'll love him too." Roxie pulled her daughter tight to her side and kissed the top of her head. "You'll see honey, this will work out just fine."

"I hope so, Mommy. I love you, and you and Aunt Katie are all I really need, you know?" Lily's blue eyes captured her mother's and Roxie felt something tug in her chest. She really loved this little girl with all her heart.

"I love you, baby. Now get some sleep. It's late, and tomorrow's a big day." Roxie tucked Lily in and turned off the bedroom light. She left the door cracked with a smile, noticing that Lily had already fallen asleep. The sleep of the innocent, if only it were that easy as an adult.

Roxie joined Aunt Katie out on the balcony, bringing

two blankets to fight off the evening chill. "It's lovely here, Roxie."

"Thanks, Aunt Katie. A friend of mine is letting me use this place for now." Roxie took a deep breath and blew it out slowly. "I can't believe this is happening."

"I thought it might happen one day," Aunt Katie said with a slight nod. "Lincoln Young was never one to let much get past him."

"No, he's not, but I thought I'd covered my tracks well. Nathan messed everything up. I knew I shouldn't have allowed that man into my life. I was so stupid." Roxie stuck her knuckles in her mouth to shut herself up and to hide the shame she felt over letting Nathan get the better of her.

"You didn't know he was a dud, honey. And maybe he wouldn't have been without the addictions, but he hid even that from you for a long time." Aunt Katie was the one who pulled Roxie into a hug this time, her chair directly to Roxie's left. "You've been my little girl since your parents hired me so many years ago, honey. I know you didn't deliberately let a man into your life who was totally wrong for you, or that would bring you so much grief. And you're not stupid at all. You were in love, and that makes us all blind sometimes."

"Not Lincoln Young," Roxie said with a snort. "Or maybe he doesn't love me. I thought he might, before all of this. I thought we were heading somewhere, but now? I'm surprised he even looks at me now."

"Give it time, things will settle down and you'll both have a talk about what's possible and what's not. I know you will. I haven't seen Lincoln for a long time, but that boy adored you when you were both teenagers. You just never noticed it because you were too busy hating him," Aunt Katie teased gently, her lips twisted up in a smile. "I saw it, don't look at me like that. He really did have it bad for you."

"I never suspected a thing," Roxie said quietly, sitting away from Aunt Katie now. "It's too late now, but maybe, if I'd known back then, I'd have made different decisions."

"Oh, you wouldn't have listened if anybody had told you that back then. You were doing only what you thought was best for Lily and Lincoln. How were you to know it was going to turn out this way, with all this animosity and anger? So many men nowadays don't want any part of fatherhood, or the responsibility, or the child support for that matter. You were doing him a favor, in a way, and saving yourself the headache of fighting him for anything." Aunt Katie contradicted herself slightly, but Roxie didn't point that out.

In a way, Aunt Katie was right though. Far too often men dodged child support, ran away when babies came along, and didn't want to be parents. Okay, so of course

Lincoln had to be different. How was Roxie to know that back then?

"That's not why I didn't tell him though," Roxie said after some thought on it all. "I've always been honest about that. I didn't want us to be a burden to him."

"I know that sweetie. I just think there's more than one side to this tale and Lincoln Young better listen or I'm going to bop him right on the nose." The tall, plump woman with large hands poked at the air in a way that might have made Lincoln's eyes water but wouldn't have done much else. "You've suffered enough. Now, honey, get to sleep. We'll sort all of this out tomorrow."

"I hope so," Roxie said and walked into the living room with Aunt Katie. They exchanged one more hug before Aunt Katie went into Roxie's bedroom. Roxie sprawled out on the couch, lost and worried about what the next day might bring to them all.

14

Roxie

"Do you want me to stay?" Nick asked and Roxie looked up at him with a frown of doubt.

"I don't think Lincoln would appreciate you being here, Nick," Roxie said from her seat on the balcony. He'd come over with breakfast for all of them, a smile on his face, but with misplaced hope in his eyes.

Roxie knew what that hope was about, but she couldn't do anything with it. Nick wasn't the man for her, a friend definitely, but not *her* man. She didn't want to lose his friendship, not for anything. Still, she couldn't seem to make him understand that friendship was all she wanted from him.

Today wasn't about him, or her even, it was about

Lincoln and Lily. That's why she'd pointed out that Lincoln wouldn't like him being there. He had to know he antagonized Lincoln, though she suspected he did it on purpose, just to annoy the other man.

"I don't care if he would appreciate it or not, Roxie. I care about you. Do you want me to stay or to leave?" Nick prompted again, and Roxie looked away, using the excuse of putting her hair up in a bun to remain quiet. "Do you, Roxie?"

"I don't think it would be a good idea, Nick. My daughter is meeting her father for the first time today. It wouldn't be fair to Lincoln. No, it's best if you leave us. He's not violent and he won't hurt me, so there's no reason for you to be here, really." Roxie looked at him, quiet strength and resolve burning in her eyes.

"I understand," Nick sighed and broke away from her eyes to stare out at the sea. "Maybe I'll take the yacht out today, get away for a little while."

"That sounds fun." Roxie let the moment pass, and brought her bare feet up to rest on the seat. "Will you do any fishing?"

It was nonsense chatter, but it kept them off the subject of Lincoln. That was just fine with Roxie.

"Maybe. I don't know. I might just go down to the strip and pretend to be a tourist for a little while. We'll see," Nick said evenly, his face unreadable now.

"Thanks for bringing breakfast. It saved me making

anything." Roxie changed the subject. Her heart was broken, she was eaten up with guilt, and getting into her feelings about anything right now wasn't her idea of a good time.

"It was my pleasure. I know how much you love French toast and coffee," Nick answered, making Roxie smile. He knew so much about her, but at the same time, so very little, she thought.

"Mommy, when is my daddy coming?" Lily asked, coming out to the balcony to stand beside her mother.

"In a little while, sweetie, don't worry. He'll be here soon." Roxie drew her daughter close with an arm around her tiny waist. "Are you excited?"

"I guess." Lily's chin was tucked down close to her chest, and she wouldn't look up. "But I like Nick. He brought me French toast and pancakes."

"I wasn't sure which you'd prefer," Nick answered, and Roxie had to squash a moment of irritation with him. "So, I got you both."

If he'd bothered to ask Roxie before he invited himself over, she'd have told him which foods Lily preferred. But that was unfair, wasn't it? Nick was trying to be helpful, not an asshole.

"Thank you, I like them both," Lily said with a grin that revealed a missing upper right incisor. Roxie almost pulled up her phone's camera to take a snapshot of her daughter's smile, to capture it forever, but resisted the urge. Lily hated having her picture taken all the time, and Roxie wanted to respect that. "Will you still be here when my daddy comes?"

Nick's eyes shot to Roxie, a plea there that she ignored, before they moved back to Lily. "No, that's special time between you and your dad. I'm going to go in a few minutes. I just need to talk to your mom a little while longer."

"Cool," Lily said with a nod that was nearly grownup. "I'm going to play on my tablet, Mom."

"That's fine, Lily. Just check the battery life first, will you?" Roxie asked, her hand on Lily's cheek with a loving smile on her face. "It's on the charger but it should be done by now."

"Sure, Mom." Lily gave a curt nod and went into the condo.

Aunt Katie came out then, interrupting Roxie as she was about to politely point out that Lincoln would be there very soon, and Nick should go. Now.

She really didn't want to seem ungrateful; Nick had given her a place to crash after all, but her nerves were already shredded. She didn't need more man-power-grunting-over-woman behavior from him or Lincoln. Lily didn't deserve that.

"I'm just wondering if you want me to stick around for this, honey? I know it's a special moment and perhaps some, ahem, privacy is in order?" Aunt Katie stood there, her face impassive, but her left eyebrow up as she faced Nick but didn't actually look at him.

Score one for the older generation, Roxie thought with an inner grin.

"That sounds good, actually," Roxie replied, her eyes on the woman who'd almost replaced her mother. Not quite, nobody could really take that place, but Aunt Katie had done a good job of filling in when Roxie needed her most. "It might be better for them both."

Nick cleared his throat, seeming to take the not-so-subtle hint Aunt Katie gave him. "I guess I should be off too, then."

Roxie stood up to see him out, thankful that he was on the way out the door now. Maybe she could hurry him along.

"Oh, what if I bring dinner over later?" Nick came to a sudden halt just as he was at the door and Roxie couldn't keep the glare from her face any longer.

"That won't be necessary, Nick. And Lincoln might want to take Lily out for dinner, or something else may come up with them. I'll figure out dinner," Roxie said with more anger in her voice than she wanted there to be.

But damn, why was he being so annoying? Or was it her, she wondered? Maybe she was just irritable about all of this.

"Of course, you're right." Nick went to open the door just as the doorbell rang.

Roxie saw Lincoln's face turn to stone as he saw Nick walking out of the condo. Luckily, Aunt Katie barged through them both and called out over her shoulder. "Nick, you can drop me off since you're leaving too. I'll see you later, Roxie."

Nick didn't say anything, he just glared at Lincoln for a moment, then moved on. Roxie breathed a silent sigh of relief and held the door open for Lincoln. "Come in."

"If you're sure your boyfriend doesn't mind," Lincoln said coldly, and Roxie had to take another deep breath to clamp down on the blunt 'fuck you' she was about to give him.

"Lincoln, you're here to meet our daughter, not comment on my private life. Please don't make me regret this." She looked at him, waiting for the moment when he either walked away or gave in and acted like a grownup.

She saw the moment he capitulated and closed the door.

"Can you, uh, can you just give me a minute, Roxie?" Lincoln asked, backing up to the door, staring up at the ceiling.

"What's wrong?" She stepped closer to him, worry flaring to life. "Are you alright?"

"I'm fine, I just," he paused, pinched the bridge of his nose, and frowned. "I just need a minute. I have a headache."

"Too much beer last night?" She asked, but without malice.

"No, just too much happening at once," he said, so low she almost didn't hear him.

She'd have asked him to elaborate but he'd made it clear she wasn't a part of his life anymore. "Want some Ibuprofen?"

"Please." He nodded and looked back down at her. For a moment, she thought she saw regret in his eyes, but then he blinked, and it was gone.

She poured him a glass of water and took two small white pills out of the economy-sized bottle she kept on hand in the cabinet. Once he'd swallowed the pills and put the glass down, she glanced into her bedroom, where Lily was happily playing Minecraft. "Give me just a minute."

Lincoln nodded and took a chair at the kitchen table. Roxie gave him a long look to check whether he was really ready for this. He looked nervous, something she wasn't used to seeing on him, but like he was ready for whatever came his way. A little girl was about to come his way, a very important one. She'd have chosen to do all of this very differently if he'd just let her speak that night, or if she'd taken a hundred different other opportunities to tell him about Lily. But none of that had happened so here they were now. This was how it had to be.

"Lily?" Roxie called out gently to her daughter. Lily was facing away from the door but rolled over when her mother called out.

"Is he here?" Lily sat up, pulling down the lilac sleeves of her long-sleeved t-shirt that she'd paired with blue jeans and multi-colored socks.

Lily hadn't inherited her mother's hatred of socks, but she had inherited her love of colors and flamboyance. "Yes, baby, he's here. Are you ready or do you need a minute?"

Lily pushed herself to the edge of the bed where her mother sat and leaned into Roxie's warmth. "Is he nice, Mommy?"

"He is, Lily. And handsome, and so, so smart. He's funny and kind, and I think you'll really like him."

"Okay. I think I'm ready." Lily took Roxie's hand and looked up into her mother's eyes.

Roxie's heart melted when she saw those blue eyes, shaped just like her father's but tinted with her eye color, and she couldn't help but hug Lily close. "No matter what baby, I love you. I will always love you, no matter where you go, or who you become when you grow up. I will always be your mother and I will always love you, just the way you are, alright?"

"I love you too, Mommy." Lily's small, thin arms wrapped around Roxie's neck as if to comfort her mother, rather than to be comforted.

Roxie was so overwhelmed with emotion that her throat closed up and she couldn't blink away tears fast enough. Lincoln must have shifted in his chair because there was a noise from the kitchen and Roxie forced herself to move away. "Come on, let's go meet your dad."

Lily didn't answer, she just smiled up at Roxie and they walked into the kitchen together. "Lincoln," Roxie called out with cheer that she didn't actually feel. "This is Lily, your daughter."

"Hi Lily,' Lincoln replied, his eyes on the little girl. "I'm so glad to meet you."

"Hi," Lily said shyly, letting her head fall so that her blonde hair hid her face. "Nice to meet you."

Roxie didn't force Lily to look up, she just took her to the other chair at the table and waited until the suddenly shy little girl sat down. "I'll just be over here on the couch, okay?"

"Okay, Mommy." Lily stared down at the table, refusing to look up.

Roxie could only assume she was being shy and looked at Lincoln. He gave a slight nod of his head, as if to accept responsibility for the girl so Roxie could go. Roxie moved over to the couch but faced the kitchen as she tucked her legs under her bottom when she sat down.

"Do you want something to drink, Lily?" Lincoln asked after a long moment of silence.

"No, thank you. I had some juice earlier," Lily answered, still not looking up.

The conversation was stilted and awkward, to the point Roxie almost broke in, but she held back. They'd agreed that he'd meet Lily first, let her get to know him, and she wouldn't intrude on that.

There'd been a lot of anger in her heart when he'd first found out, but that had mainly been over the way he came at her with the newly discovered information. It had stung that he'd thought so little of her, that he'd treated her so badly. Now she could understand that anger and just wanted to build a bridge that would allow them to co-parent together. The alternative was that he'd take Lily away from her and she'd never see her daughter again. She couldn't handle that, at all. Somehow she had to get through this, for Lily's sake.

"Your mom tells me you like music and ballet," Lincoln said after another long silence. "I play piano."

"You do?" Lily said with happiness. "I love piano, but the violin is my favorite. And I want to learn cello too."

"You'll be a one-girl band before it's done with," Lincoln laughed, the sound tense but not as tense as he was before. "I started playing piano when I was very young. My mom plays too."

"Does she?" Lily asked and then paused before she spoke again. "That's my grandmother, right?"

"Yes, she's your grandmother," Lincoln said gently, but Roxie could hear the unspoken 'though she doesn't know it yet'.

Roxie had a moment of panic as she thought about Ms. Young, Lincoln's mother. She was always Ms. Young to her children's friends, and Roxie could still remember the way the woman would stare coldly down at her at times. Roxie hadn't often acted up as a child, but accidents happened, and Roxie could clearly remember a very ugly vase being broken that Ms. Young had been very upset about. It was probably worth more than Roxie's car, but she still had no idea what the broken vase had actually cost.

At other times Ms. Young was fun, took part in activities with the kids, and made them all laugh. Roxie had a feeling there was a lot more to the woman than even her children knew about. She tried to imagine Lincoln's mother as a grandmother and couldn't fathom it.

"Can I meet her?" Lily asked, breaking into Roxie's thoughts.

"Sure, when you're ready. When she's back from, um, wherever she is at the moment." Lincoln's face showed confusion and Roxie had a feeling that was because he had no idea where his mother was.

"Is she on vacation?" Lily asked, looking up at her father at last. Her shyness was fading finally and that made Lincoln smile.

"Probably. She spends a lot of time in different places."

"Cool. Can we go down to the playground? There's one just down there." Lily pointed behind her, at the balcony doors, meaning out by the beach.

"Sure, we can do that." Lincoln looked down at his suit and the polished leather shoes he wore. He looked back up and Roxie knew he'd decided it didn't matter if the sand scuffed his expensive shoes or if they messed up his clothes. Spending time with Lily was more important than any of those things.

Roxie watched, certain now that things would be alright. At least they would be between Lily and Lincoln. How things would turn out between mother and father she had no clue, but at least her daughter would have her father, at last. That was good enough.

15

Lincoln

Lincoln was aware that Roxie was behind them on a park bench as he pushed Lily on a swing. He knew he looked calm, even happy, on the outside, but inside he was in turmoil. This was one of the happiest days of his life, he had just met his daughter and he was already in love.

The problem was Lily's mother. Roxie's face went from terrified, to happy, to angry every time he stole a glance at her. He couldn't imagine what she must be thinking, and she wasn't talking so it wasn't likely that he'd find out either. He'd really upset her the last few times they'd seen each other and part of him regretted that.

There were much better ways to handle the situation he'd found himself in, he should have given her the benefit of the doubt, but he hadn't. He'd stomped all over her feelings, treated her terribly, and had then insulted her on top of all that. To be fair, it was a surprise that she was allowing this at all, after his threat to take Lily away from her.

He still planned to claim his daughter and ask for custody of her, but that was for Lily's protection, not to get back at Roxie. When he'd first told her that was his plan, he'd spoken in anger and with a need to hurt. He'd wanted to see her in as much pain as he'd been in at that moment.

Now he just wanted to protect the little girl who'd been so shy when they first met. But once she'd figured out he wasn't an ogre she'd started to talk. He now knew that she had a dozen favorite colors, that her best friend was named Millie, and that she hated boys because they were always picking their noses. She liked all kinds of music and her favorite things to watch were documentaries and an old television show Aunt Katie liked called *Bewitched*.

Lincoln told her his favorite color was the blue shade of her eyes, and when she asked what his favorite dog was, he told her that his favorite was the beagle, even though he didn't have a dog.

"But you're a grownup, you can do what you want. Why don't you have a dog?" Lily asked, dragging her feet on the ground to slow down and turn back to look at him.

"Well, my mother never allowed pets in the house, and I move around a lot too, so it wouldn't be fair to the dog really. It would have to travel a lot." Lincoln was making the excuses up on the fly, but now that he thought about it, he wondered why he didn't have a dog. His mom hadn't even allowed one of those expensive, decorative cats in the house when he was a kid. When he grew up, it hadn't occurred to him that he could have a pet at last.

"I'm sure a dog would love to see the places you go to," Lily said, as if she knew all the inner thoughts of a dog's mind. She was a smart kid so maybe she did, he thought with a smile. "Dogs like to be with their humans."

"They do, yes." Lincoln decided he'd have one of his PAs start looking for a suitable puppy. When Lily came to live with him, a dog might help her settle in.

"And what's your favorite food?" Lily asked, which set off a million other questions.

"All of it, really," Lincoln answered, and she settled back into the swing for more pushing.

"Do I have to call you dad?" She asked once they'd started to make their way back inside.

Lincoln's footsteps faltered but he caught back up with her. "No. You don't have to if you don't want to, yet. You can call me Lincoln."

"Alright." She nodded, happy enough, and put her hand in his.

He felt something warm and breathtaking in his chest with that minor show of trust. He wasn't Dad to her yet, but that was okay. Time would mend everything between father and child. He hoped.

By the time the sun started to settle in the sky Lincoln was questioned out but not ready to end the day. He glanced over at Roxie, watching something on the TV now that they'd come back inside. She had the subtitles on so she wouldn't disturb the game of Uno he'd been playing with Aunt Katie and Lily.

"Can I take you all out for dinner, Roxie?" He asked, after observing her for a moment. She was engrossed in whatever it was she was watching but looked over with her eyebrows raised when he spoke.

"What?" For a moment, a smile lingered at the corners of her mouth, but then it disappeared. "Oh, food. Sure, if Lily wants to go somewhere."

"Can't we just order something, Mommy?" Lily left the game to come and sprawl out against her mom's legs. "I'm tired."

"It's up to your dad, I guess, Lily. Ask him." Roxie brushed hair away from Lily's face, gently tweaking her daughter's earlobe which made Lily giggle and sit up.

"Can we do that, Lincoln?" Lily asked, using the name they'd agreed to use until she was comfortable with something else. Lincoln really wanted to hear her call him dad, but now he knew that when he did hear it, he'd have earned the title.

"Sure, what do you want?" He waited for an answer, certain she'd say pizza, but she surprised him.

"Tacos!" She cried out happily and ran to him to bounce on her feet in excitement. "The ones with sour cream, please. And some chips and salsa, and guacamole, don't forget that."

"You are your mother's daughter," Lincoln laughed and pulled up a food ordering app on his phone. "What does everybody else want?"

"I'll just have a sandwich and go to bed, but thank you, Lincoln. It's been a long day and I'm a little tired." Aunt Katie got up from the table and Lincoln watched her, wondering if she was alright.

"Are you okay?" He asked softly, and she turned to nod at him.

"I'm fine, I'm just 74. I'm not a spring chicken anymore. If I ate tacos at this time of night my stomach would make me pay dearly for it. Enjoy your dinner, I'll be fine."

"Alright, but if you want anything, just let me know."

Lincoln turned to look at Roxie and he was surprised to catch her watching him, studying him really. Her face smoothed out the instant he turned to her, but he'd caught the look on her face. She approved of how he'd treated Katie then.

"As you said, I'm your daughter's mother. I'll have the same thing she's having." Roxie added to the order he was building but didn't move from the couch.

He'd really like it if she'd come and sit with them at the table, but it had been clear all day she was leaving him to get to know his daughter. She stayed close, in case Lily wanted her, but she'd left him to get on with getting to know Lily.

By the time the food arrived, and they'd all eaten, Lily's eyelids were starting to droop. She'd had a shower while they waited for the food and now she was quickly falling asleep on the floor in front of the couch. She'd settled down there to play videos on her tablet while Roxie and Lincoln finished eating.

"I'll put her to bed," Roxie said and got up from the table. "Say goodnight to Lincoln, honey."

"Good night, Dad," Lily called out, a yawn interrupting the word dad, but he heard it. That was enough, for now.

Roxie came back in a few minutes later and started to clear away their garbage. "She's out like a light."

"It was a long day for both of us, I guess." Lincoln

stacked up empty bottles of water in the bag she'd pulled out from under the sink and held out for him. "Has she got any health problems?"

"No, why?" Roxie had started to move away but stopped. "Would that change anything?"

"No, I just wanted to know. If she needed some kind of care, I wanted to make sure I knew about it. That's all."

"She's a healthy 9-year-old girl, who sometimes has way too much energy and a million questions about everything, but that's normal too." Roxie finished clearing up the table and put the bag by the door before she sat back down. "As far as I know, she has no major health problems, though her dentist is trying to convince Aunt Katie she'll need braces."

"We'll get her a dentist here." Lincoln dismissed the New York dentist and went on to his next question. "When are they going back?"

"Well, I don't know yet. I'm going to talk to Lily tomorrow and find out what she feels. She likes the idea of being able to see me whenever she wants to, but I don't think she realizes what she'll be leaving behind in New York if they come down here." Roxie's lips pulled in for a minute but then relaxed. "I would like to have her here, where I can be near to her, see her when I want to, but it's up to her. We aren't giving her a lot of choices at the moment, but this part has to be her decision."

"I agree," he mumbled, thinking about when he was nine and how many places he'd lived by then. He didn't want to drag her all over the country the way he'd been moved about like baggage. "If she wants to stay down here, I'll do what I have to."

"Thank you. And thank you for promising I can see her when I want to." Roxie didn't look at him, instead, she got up and took a bottle of white wine from the fridge. "Do you want a glass?"

"No, I'll be going in a few minutes. I just wanted to say, well, thank you for today. I didn't like the idea at first, but it makes sense. She has to know who I am before I force her to live with me. And Aunt Katie as well." Lincoln tapped a manicured finger against the table and wondered what his next move should be. "If she wants to stay down here, we'll find them a bigger place to stay temporarily."

"That might be better," Roxie conceded. "This wouldn't have been my first choice of place to bring her to, but my apartment is even smaller."

"I know, that's why I thought a bigger place might be better." That and she wouldn't have to see Nick if she wasn't here, he thought. But then another thought struck. "Um, what if I find somewhere else and you go to my place with them?"

"Oh." Roxie leaned against the couch, took a sip of her wine, and then stared down into the glass. "She'd be used to your house by then. The only change would be you'd come to stay later, and I'd leave."

"Yes," Lincoln said, trying to ignore how sad it made him to hear that she'd leave again. That had been his choice, though, hadn't it? Even if he did regret it now.

"That would work." Roxie nodded and looked up from her wine finally. "I'll talk to Aunt Katie in the morning."

"Good. I guess I'll be off then." He stood up, looked around one last time, and put his hands in his pockets. "You'll call me tomorrow?"

"Yeah, sure." Roxie didn't move from the couch, she just took another sip of her wine, staring out towards the balcony. For a moment, Lincoln wanted to go over, take the glass from her, throw it against the wall and pull her into his arms. He wanted to tell her he'd made a huge mistake and he regretted it. But she was in another man's condo, and clearly didn't want him near her. She hadn't even moved to walk him out the door.

She was still upset. He'd have to live with that.

"Alright, talk to you then." He opened the door, ready to go, but he stopped and turned back to her before he closed it. "Good night, Roxie."

"Good night, Lincoln." He heard her say but she didn't look up.

He'd hurt her deeply, and now they were both living with the consequences.

She'd looked so lonely, leaning against that couch, he almost went back in to beg her to forgive him. But maybe she'd moved on. Nick had been there when he'd arrived earlier, had he stayed the night with her?

Lincoln couldn't see her having a man over when her daughter had only just arrived, but what did he know? Maybe she needed the comfort the other man could give her.

Lincoln wanted to smash something but knew it wouldn't accomplish anything. And he'd end up in jail if that something was Nick's smug face. The bastard.

The house was dark - he'd forgotten to leave any lights on when he left earlier - and far too quiet to be comfortable. Lincoln turned on some music and opened a bottle of beer once he'd changed into some pajamas. Sitting at the kitchen table, he opened his laptop and started looking for a short-term rental property.

If Lily needed some time to get to know him, he'd give it to her. He might know nothing about being a father, but he knew a lot about how to not treat a child. She'd get love, attention, and respect from him for the rest of her life. If that meant he had to rent out a place for himself for a little while so she could get used to his house, so be it.

For a moment, he thought about telling Roxie that he wanted to stay, that she should just come over for a little while and go back to her place once Lily was settled in.

But that would backfire in an instant. There were too many memories of happier times in the house. Memories that would complicate the situation more than it already was.

16

Roxie

"So, she's out with Lincoln now?" Wendy asked as she helped Roxie pack up her stuff to take to Lincoln's.

"Yeah, he offered to take her to his house while I got everything packed. Aunt Katie is with them," Roxie answered automatically, her mind a million miles away.

"What's wrong?" Wendy asked from the door of the bathroom, staring out as Roxie folded clothes and put them in a suitcase instead of the dryer.

"I guess it's Lincoln, in general. I messed up and he won't forgive me. I can't blame him, really," Roxie replied, putting one of Lily's dresses in the suitcase. "Now, I have to go live in his house again. Do you realize how many times I've moved in the last few months? And I still have the apartment."

"I wish I could help. Do you need me to bring anything from the apartment? I know you may end up back there, but just in case, do you want me to bring anything?"

Roxie smiled for the first time since Lincoln picked up Lily and Katie earlier that day. "Yeah, actually, I do. There's a secret hiding space in the floor, I have a few things in there, a note, some lip gloss, I'd like to have with me. They're just mementos, but I don't want to lose them."

"Notes and lip gloss? What's that about?" Wendy asked, going back to placing toiletries in a plastic shopping bag.

"It's just stuff from my childhood," Roxie answered vaguely, on purpose. She didn't want to talk about it and Wendy let it go, thankfully.

"I swear, I'm moving in there when you finally do move out," Wendy joked, but Roxie had to wonder if she actually meant it. "You know, I think you'd be safe if you moved back in there."

Wendy let the words trail off and Roxie looked at her with a puzzled look. "What do you mean?"

"Well, I have a connection. There's someone watching the place all the time now."

"I'm aware of the under-the-table stuff that happens

at Lemon Fresh, Wendy. It's one of the reasons I chose the place. It's like there's this invisible force protecting the place because of whatever business it is your parents are involved in." Roxie shrugged, then went on. "It's a force not to be messed with and I'm sure your parents stepped up security since all the shit with Nathan happened."

"You're right, they have. They miss you, you know?" Wendy said, sniffing a bottle of shampoo before putting it in the bag and coming out of the bathroom. "I'm all done in there. I can't see anything else that needs to go."

"What is it your parents are actually doing, Wendy?" Roxie stopped folding clothes and looked over at her friend to see her holding out a hand, palm up.

"I don't know any more than you do. I just know that there's an agreement between my grandfather and some other guy. They saved each other's life back in the day and they look out for each other now. That's carried over to my dad and that's about all I know." Wendy put the bag with the rest of Roxie's stuff by the door and sighed. "What else can we do?"

"You can tell me if they have any dealings with people in New York," Roxie said carefully, an idea forming. Maybe she could find out who it was that had been after her parents and put a stop to all of this. End the hiding, the worry, and finally be able to live a normal life. Maybe even go back to her old name.

Wendy turned around slowly, her face an unreadable mask. "I don't think you want to mess with anybody from New York, Rox. They're the real deal up there and not to be fucked with. Seriously, don't go looking for more trouble than you already have."

"I'm not, just trying to see if there's a way to deal with some of the trouble that I already have, as you pointed out." Roxie closed the empty dryer and zipped up the suitcase. "I just thought I'd ask."

"Sorry, I'm not used to talking about any of that, you know?" Wendy rolled her eyes at herself and came to hug Roxie. "I'm sorry I can't help you with whatever that's about. Those are dangerous people, seriously."

"I know and thank you for looking out for me." Roxie withdrew from the hug and put her right hand against Wendy's tanned face. "You're a good friend. I'm so glad I have you."

"I'm glad you do too," Wendy joked with a laugh and went to sit on the couch. "So, tell me more about this Nick guy. Are you in some kind of love triangle with him and Lincoln?"

"Nooooo!" Roxie protested and sat down with her friend, her hands hiding her face. "Nick would love to replace Lincoln. Lincoln's finished with me, and I'm just bouncing around from place to place, trying to find my anchor again. Lincoln's the man I want, but he doesn't want me anymore. Nick is a really good friend, and he'd make someone a really good husband, but I'm not ready for anybody after all of this shit with Lincoln."

"So why's he single? If you've made it clear you don't want him, why's he hanging around, giving you a place to stay, all of that?" Wendy prodded, but not with malice. She only wanted to understand the situation better.

"I'm not leading him on if that's what you think," Roxie sighed, sitting back to look at Wendy with a face filled with sadness. "I've tried to make him understand I'm not the one for him, but he keeps hanging on, hoping I'll change my mind. He tries to keep it at the friend level, but sometimes he oversteps that line. I don't know what to do about it."

"What if Lincoln doesn't come around? Would Nick be an option?" Wendy poked a little further, a tiny smile curling the corners of her mouth up.

"I don't think so. I mean he's hot, smart, kind and so considerate," Roxie paused as if confused about why she didn't find him attractive in a romantic way. "He's a catch really, but there's something missing for me."

"Danger maybe? Or wild sex? Or you're just not that into him?" Wendy teased again, pulling at Roxie's right hand with her own. "Whatever the reason, you know what you want and don't want. He has to respect that."

"He does, and he tries, but sometimes I'm just on the verge of screaming at him to stop it," Roxie admitted, tightening her grip on Wendy's hand. "Why are men such morons sometimes?"

"The same reasons we are, I guess." Wendy rolled her eyes again before she continued. "I mean, we do a lot of stupid shit sometimes too, us women."

"We do. Like fall in love with men that don't want to be near us anymore," Roxie answered quietly, as if she really didn't want Wendy to hear, but Roxie knew she had when sadness clouded Wendy's brown eyes.

"I'm sorry, my friend. I wish I could fix that. But the way you explained it, it made sense to me. I mean, you could have gone after him for child support and everything, but you didn't. Most men would be happy about that." Wendy dropped Roxie's hand and pushed her black hair behind her shoulders. "You wanted to keep Lily safe, how can he not understand that?"

"He's been through a lot lately," Roxie protested, but Wendy shook her head.

"No, don't make excuses for him. He has been through a lot but so have you, for a very long time, in fact. Hopefully, he'll come around and see the light. If not, fuck him. Nobody's good enough for you as far as I'm concerned anyway." Wendy grinned and pulled Roxie in for another hug.

Roxie lost it then and tears formed in her eyes. Wendy loved her so much and that love overwhelmed her defenses. Sobs tore from Roxie's throat as she let some of the pain she felt, the guilt she held, and Lincoln's rejection all come flooding out.

Wendy held on, bless her, not letting go as Roxie's tears flowed freely and she clung to her. "I can't believe this is happening."

"I know, honey. I can't either, and when I see him again, I'm kicking him in the balls so hard he'll never be able to get his dick up again, not without needing a crank of some kind," Wendy said with vicious glee. "He won't be able to fuck another woman ever again without thinking of me."

"Oh, don't do that." Roxie gave a watery laugh and pulled away, wiping at her face with a tissue from the box on the table in front of her. "Just breaking his jaw might be better. Then he won't be able to tell another woman he loves her or anything else."

"I like that," Wendy said and gave Roxie a questioning look. "Are you okay?"

"No, but I will be," Roxie answered and stood up. "We can't sit here all day fantasizing about what we'd do with Lincoln. I need to get over to the house and make sure Lily's settled in."

"She's fine, Roxie. Katie is with her and so is Lincoln. Let her have some time with her dad. You need some time to get used to this new living situation too, you know?"

"I know." Roxie heaved a sigh and let her head fall back. "I can't believe I'm going back there without him."

"That's exactly what I mean." Wendy pursed her lips and frowned at Roxie. "If he hurts you again, I really will crush his balls, Rox. I'm not joking."

"I don't think there's much chance of that, Wendy. He's already got a temporary place. I'll stay at the house for a few weeks, let Lily get used to it all, and then go back to my place above Lemon Fresh. He's interested in getting to know his daughter, not rekindling a relationship with her mother. Romance is not in the cards."

"I really hate that for you. I know how much you care about him." Wendy looked away, her own eyes a little shiny now. "When he was missing, it became obvious just how much you feel about him. Knowing he's broken it off with you is so sad."

"I can't force him to forgive me. I can't make him love me. I thought, for a while, that maybe he did, you know? That I was different and maybe there was something more in store for us, but it's over and I have to face facts. I'm nothing more than Lily's mother and that's all."

"I'm so sorry, Roxie," Wendy said with evident regret in her voice. "I was really hoping it would work out for you two."

"That's life, right?" Roxie swiped at her face with another tissue and took a deep breath. "I'm a big girl, I'll get back to my business, see my daughter more often, and somehow, I'll get over all of this. I don't know how, but I will."

"You will. I'll be there for you," Wendy said, and Roxie knew she would be.

"Well, let's get out of here before Nick comes back and tries to convince me to stay. He's not happy I'm going back to Lincoln's." Roxie got up, swiped a hand over her bun to make sure her hair was in place, and breathed deeply again. "That was a conversation I don't want to have to repeat."

"I bet," Wendy answered as she got up and pushed down the dark blue silk dress she wore, smoothing the lines until the dress came down to her knees in a pretty flare. "Was he a dick to you?"

"Not to me, but he was angry. He mentioned Lincoln's balls too, in fact." Roxie grinned and slipped on a pair of loafers. She was dressed in blue jeans and a black slouchy blouse for comfort, not to impress. "I thought I'd have to call the police to go over to Lincoln's and protect him."

"Oh no, that would have been bad." Wendy winced but grabbed up plastic bags in one hand and a suitcase handle in the other. "Got the keys?"

"Yes, I'm leaving them in the mailbox. He has the key for that." Roxie grabbed her purse, two suitcases, and looked around one last time to make sure she hadn't left anything. "At least I wasn't here long enough to get settled in."

"I'd miss that view," Wendy said as she opened the door. "But that's about all."

"I'll have all the ocean I can stand at Lincoln's place. For a little while at least," Roxie answered, closing the door and making sure it was locked behind her. "Let's go."

She dropped the keys off while Wendy loaded Roxie's car. When Roxie came back Wendy gave her another hug and looked at her carefully before she let go. "You know I'm only a text message away, right?"

"I do, and the same goes for you," Roxie replied, meaning it. "You've done so much for me already, I feel bad asking you for more help."

"Anytime you need me, Roxie, ask. I'm more than happy to help." Wendy dug around in her own handbag and pulled out her keys. "I'd better get back to the shop. Mom and Dad will be wondering where I am."

"Thanks, Wendy, for everything." Roxie waved as Wendy started to walk backwards towards her car.

Wendy waved and turned around, getting into her car without another word.

Roxie watched her friend pull out of the parking garage with sad eyes and a broken heart. She'd been able to keep the tears at bay for a little while and it was nice that Wendy was there for her when the walls cracked a little. But now, standing there alone, wondering what the hell fate had in store for her next, Roxie almost got in the car to drive far away and leave it all behind.

Lily had her father now, Lincoln had his daughter, and he'd keep her safe. Meanwhile, the only thing that would make Roxie smile from now on was her daughter. She had to live in a house filled with memories of him, had to smell his scent in the air, and look at him without being able to touch him or love him.

Roxie saw a future as a shell ahead of her and that nearly made her run away. But she couldn't leave her daughter. Not ever again.

17

Roxie

 efore she could even start her car, there was
a tap at her window that made Roxie jump
and scream. She was furious when she saw it was Nick,
standing there with a confused smile on his face.

"What made you jump like that, it's just me?" He
asked, opening her car door. "I thought you might need
a hand loading your stuff up, then saw you sitting here
in the car. Are you alright?"

"I'm fine," she said with a pissed-off snip in her voice.
"You just scared the ever-loving shit out of me. Holy
fuck."

With her right hand over her chest, Roxie tried to
calm down her racing heart.

"Sorry, after all you've been through, I should have

known better than to do that." Nick stood up to let Roxie get out of the small SUV and opened his arms, expecting a hug.

Roxie felt bad about being so angry with him and hugged him back. "It's alright, you didn't mean anything by it."

It felt nice to be in his arms, he was her friend after all, and he smelled good. Roxie relaxed as she stood there, wishing she could give him the relationship he wanted. But Lincoln's face floated into her mind, and she pulled away.

"I'm all packed up, ready to go." She was still in his arms, and she could see it on his face, he was going to kiss her. Stunned, she just stood there, letting his warm lips touch hers without protest. Maybe if she let it happen, she'd feel something for him?

Which was exactly when Lincoln pulled up in his car behind them, his face a mask of fury.

"Fuck," Roxie whispered, pulling away completely now, her irritation and anxiety on full alert.

"I came by to see if you needed a hand with your belongings. I guess you have your hands full already," Lincoln said when he stepped out of the car and glared with malice at Nick.

"Don't be rude, Lincoln. This is Nick's place. He has a right to be here and he was just saying goodbye."

"That didn't look like goodbye to me," Lincoln

muttered, his eyes on Roxie now, hurt dwelling some-where in the angry depths but she knew that hurt wouldn't be there for long. She was right and knew it when Nick spoke up, making it a thousand times worse.

"What happens between Roxie and I is none of your business, Lincoln."

The hurt disappeared, replaced with a simmering rage. "Shut the fuck up, Nick. You have no say in what I do or don't do."

"Actually, this is Nick's property, Lincoln, and he does have a say. Besides, he's not the one who's had somebody tailing me for the last couple of days." Roxie brought up the one subject she'd tried to ignore because she wasn't sure if it meant Lincoln still cared about her or if he was just trying to get dirt on her.

"What? What the hell are you talking about?" Lincoln turned to her, real confusion scrunching his face up.

"The PI or one of the guys from your boy's club that's been following me around everywhere I go without you. It's kind of rude, Lincoln."

"I can't believe you have someone following her. That's fucked up, man," Nick added, disgust written all over his face. "You're the one that told her to get out, why would you do something like that if you're done with her?"

"I don't have anyone tailing you, it must be your imagination after everything that's happened." Lincoln dismissed the whole thing and went back to his car. He glared at Nick, a threat on his face that he didn't verbalize.

Roxie didn't like the way Lincoln's jealousy made her feel, like she had a chance of getting him back, because she knew she was just a toy to Lincoln. One he'd thrown away. The only reason he was jealous now was because someone else wanted to play with her. Fuck that.

"Fuck, I fucking hate you, Lincoln," she hissed. "Nick is a very good friend to me and you're over here acting like the biggest dick ever created. Stop it. Just go back to the fucking house, I'll be there soon."

"Sure. Whatever, Roxie," Lincoln answered with a sneer that made her want to slap him. Why was he being such an asshole?

Lincoln got in his car and sped off without another look. Roxie slumped back down into the car and looked at Nick. "I don't know how I'm going to get through this. He's acting like a child."

"He's just regretting a very stupid decision, Rox. He'll calm down," Nick responded, shocking her with his insight. "He still cares, he's just being a massive dick because he doesn't know what to do about it."

"That's a strange thing for you to say," she replied, wondering at the sudden change in his attitude.

"I know you care about him, Roxie. And I know he's broken your heart. I wish it wasn't so, but it is. All I can do now is try to help you get through the part that comes next. It's a strange situation and you're all going to have a lot to deal with. I've been acting like a chump myself, trying to convince you to be with me. I've been a dick too, and I'm sorry."

"It's fine, Nick." Roxie dismissed the apology but took his words to heart. She needed a friend and he'd realized that finally.

"Well, I saw the way you looked at him, like you wanted to explain why I'd just kissed you and how it didn't matter. That's pretty definitive proof that I've been overstepping, and you aren't ready for anything from me. I'll try to stop that from now on."

"Thanks. I guess I should go now." Roxie didn't turn to start the car though. "If I'm honest though, I'm not sure I want to go anywhere."

"If you want, we can go across the street, get some coffee. As friends. You don't have to do this alone, you know?" Nick leaned against the open door nonchalantly, not a threat at all, just a concerned friend.

Roxie considered the offer, looked out of her windshield, and really thought about what she was about to do. Lily would be out of her control, really out of her control. Lincoln would see to that, no matter how she might fight him. He'd use her career, her past, her lack of riches against her. This stupid plan of his was the only way to ensure she had some kind of interaction with her daughter in the future.

"It'll be fine, Nick. I'll give you a call soon, let you know how it's going, alright?" She said, feeling something broken inside shatter a little bit more. "I should go."

"Okay, Roxie. But just know, I'm here if you need me."

Roxie smiled and closed the door. Everybody that she felt she could count on had said those words to her a dozen times lately. She knew they meant them, too, but none of them could help her. Not against Lincoln Young.

Roxie started the car and drove away, leaving Nick in the parking garage. The sun was about to set, and she saw the lights of a dozen bars. The urge to pull into one and sit with a bottle of tequila until she couldn't feel anything hit her hard. So hard, she pulled into one and sat in the parking lot.

People passed all around, into the bar, further down to other places, none of them knowing or caring about the turmoil boiling inside of her. Roxie wasn't one to drown her sorrows in alcohol, but she wanted that numbness right now. She wanted to forget about everything and lose the sensation that her soul was being crushed, for just a little while.

Yeah, she'd have a hangover from hell tomorrow, and

she might end up puking all over wherever or whoever she ended up with, but it might just be worth it. But she'd be leaving Lily in that new house without her there. Lily would spend her first night in a strange house with only Katie there to comfort her.

Being a full-time mother wasn't something Roxie had been for most of Lily's life, and it wouldn't be now. But she could be the best part-time mom Lincoln would allow her to be. Putting the car back into drive, Roxie drove out of the parking lot and made her way to Lincoln's house.

The lights were on in the house when she got there, a sight that made Roxie smile. She loved this house, loved the people inside of it now, waiting on her. Once the engine was turned off, Roxie got out and stared at the house. She hadn't expected to ever walk back through that door, but here she was, a new chapter in a story that had been fractured but calm, until Lincoln Young came back into her life.

It would be great having Lily so close from now on, but at what price? Could she really do this?

"It won't be so bad, Roxie," Lincoln's voice came out of the shadows around the porch, startling her.

"You say that like you have any clue what's going on inside my head, Lincoln." She moved away from the SUV, checking to make sure the security gate had slid closed behind her. Taking each step slowly, she walked up to him and looked down at a man who was as unknowable as he'd been the first day she saw him again after their long separation.

"I know you very well, Roxie. More than you think." He stood and looked down at her. His face was unreadable and not just because it was dark on the porch. He'd closed off. "We'll manage this if you can keep it together."

"I'm not going to fall apart just because you dumped me, Lincoln. I've had worse pain in my life." She dismissed him and turned to open the door.

"I've said good night to Lily. See you tomorrow." Lincoln stepped off the porch with a wave. "Goodnight."

"Goodnight, Lincoln," she said, wishing silently that dreams of her making him come a thousand different ways would haunt him all night. Asshole.

"Mommy, you're here! The beach is just outside!" Lily cried as soon as Roxie closed the door, running to hug her mother's legs.

"I know baby, isn't it a beautiful house?" Roxie took Lily's hand and headed to the kitchen, the place where she'd spent so much of her time, before Lincoln ended things with her.

"It's my favorite house ever!" Lily cried and went to stand on the back deck. "I want to live here forever."

"Well, luckily, your father agrees." Roxie smiled at

her daughter's enthusiasm, even though her heart ached terribly.

"I've got a chicken casserole in the oven, Roxie. Are you hungry?" Aunt Katie asked as she came into the kitchen, a faint smile on her face.

"I am, yeah," Roxie said, even though she wasn't. She'd eat to keep Katie from worrying. Besides, Katie's chicken casserole was heavenly, even when you didn't want to eat.

"Good, it's almost done. This is a nice house. And Lincoln's already sat down and ordered everything Lily wants in her bedroom," the older woman said carefully, watching Roxie closely.

Roxie smiled appropriately, hiding the fact that she just wanted to sleep and forget all of this existed. Which brought to mind a new question…where was she sleeping? It dawned on her then that she'd have to sleep in Lincoln's room. All the other rooms were occupied now. For fuck's sake.

The smile on Roxie's face became brittle but didn't slip. "I can't wait. Honey, come back inside, it's getting cold now."

Lily came back in and chattered through dinner, telling Roxie all about the new things Lincoln had bought for her and the plans they'd made together. Roxie nodded at each new detail, glad that Lincoln was taking to fatherhood so enthusiastically, but wondering when she'd have time with her daughter at the same time.

"I have to start school down here and find new teachers for my dance and music lessons, but that's okay."

"Well, surely you could teach her dance until we find someone else, couldn't you, Roxie?" Aunt Katie broke into the stream of words Lily had been speaking and Roxie blinked at her, lost for a moment.

She couldn't teach her daughter how to be a pole dancer, not yet anyway. Then it dawned on her. "Oh, the ballet? Well, yes, I suppose I could."

A broken shard deep in her soul suddenly joined back to another and light filtered in through the darkness. It would be wonderful to teach Lily in the studio upstairs. What a lovely idea. For those moments, she could have her daughter close, teach her, and do something else she loved dearly…dance.

"Really, Mommy? I've never seen you dance," Lily asked, looking a little doubtful.

"No, there wasn't anywhere for me to dance in New York, but there's a studio upstairs. Did your father show it to you?" Roxie asked, smiling at Aunt Katie when she picked up the now empty dishes from the table.

"No, can you show me?" Lily asked, sitting straight up with excitement.

"Sure, honey. After we help Aunt Katie with the dishes." Roxie reminded the little girl that they needed to help clean up and smiled when Lily's face fell.

"Don't worry, there's a dishwasher and I don't mind clearing everything away. Also, um, Roxie, there's a lot of eyes around, keeping watch on us. I didn't know if you knew," Aunt Katie said that last part carefully and very quietly.

"Oh yes, I had a feeling there were," Roxie answered with a nod. "If you're sure you can handle this, I'll take her upstairs."

"Sure, I'll be fine." Aunt Katie nodded and started to load the dishwasher. "Spend some time with your daughter, honey. I've got this."

"Thanks, Aunt Katie. For everything." Roxie went over and kissed the wrinkled cheek of the only mother figure she had now. "You're more special than you know."

"Well, so are you, my dear. Go on now, have fun." Katie patted Roxie's cheek and went back to the dishwasher.

"Do you have any dance outfits for me here?" Lily asked as they walked up the stairs, hand in hand.

"No, but we'll get you some," Roxie said, ignoring the door with the padlock on it, even though memories called to her with a fierce tug that nearly took her breath away.

"I can't wait. Oh, Mommy, this is beautiful," Lily

cried as soon as Roxie turned on the lights of the studio. "I can't believe I have my own studio."

Roxie didn't tell Lily that her father built the studio for her mother, there was no reason to burst the child's bubble. Besides, it wasn't hers anymore, was it? and it never would be. Blinking away her tears, Roxie let her daughter run around the studio, holding herself together with tiny threads that hadn't broken yet, but just might if she wasn't careful. She'd have to be very careful, for Lily's sake. Lily was all that mattered now.

Roxie

ily was so excited to be living in a new place, with a father that she hadn't known existed, that when she got up the next morning, she didn't complain about starting at a new school. Roxie was surprised, she'd thought Lily would be nervous, maybe even a little unhappy to have left her friends behind. Instead, Lily came down to breakfast with a smile on her face, her hair in a ponytail, dressed in a blue skirt and white shirt that was the uniform of the school Lincoln had insisted they enroll her in.

He'd somehow managed to arrange it all over the weekend. The man had connections, that was certain.

"Are you ready for your first day at the new school?" Roxie asked, wanting to be sure Lily was alright.

"I'm excited. I'll make new friends and have new teachers. I'll miss my old friends, but it's good to meet new people, right?" Lily said with far more wisdom than a nine-year-old should have.

"I suppose it is, yes. Well, you have my phone number if you need me, and your father's." Roxie frowned as she took the empty plates away. Lily seemed to be dealing with this much better than she was.

"Dad is meeting me at the school with Aunt Katie. She's got to sign some papers or something." Lily wasn't concerned about that part; she didn't understand that Roxie had given Aunt Katie the right to care for Lily a long time ago. Luckily, Aunt Katie had been smart enough to bring all the necessary paperwork with her when she left New York.

"I see," Roxie said, wondering how long she was going to be alone in this house for. It didn't make sense to stay here all day if everyone was gone, but where else did she have to go?

"Are you ready, sweetheart?" Aunt Katie called out as she came into the kitchen, dressed in a pair of black slacks with a green long-sleeved blouse. Her gray hair was up in a bun, matronly but still somehow soft.

Roxie smiled and looked over at her with a knowing smile. "Lily's much readier than I am, it seems."

"She's always been a brave girl," Aunt Katie whispered. "Much like her mother."

Roxie put her right hand on Aunt Katie's shoulder in thanks. "I appreciate you taking her in and getting everything signed. I'm sure Lincoln will soon have that all sorted so he can take over those responsibilities."

"I'm sure he will," Aunt Katie agreed, frowning for a moment. "He means well, Roxie."

"I know he does." Roxie moved away to wash the few plates and glasses in the sink.

"I do too, honey. But you know, I will always do what's best for Lily." The older woman looked away; her eyes filled with sadness. "It's a hard place for all of us to be."

"It is. That's enough of that for one morning." Roxie plastered a fake smile on her face and lifted her head up. "You two get to school. Have a good day, Lily. I hope you make lots of new friends."

"I love you, Mommy," Lily said as she rushed to wrap her arms around her mother's hips. "You'll be here when I get home?"

"Of course I will, darling. I'll be right here waiting for you." Roxie bent down to kiss Lily on the top of the head. "Now go on, you don't want to be late."

"I don't. 'Bye, Mommy," Lily called, running to the hallway to grab her book bag and put her shoes on.

"I'll see you later, Roxie. Try to stay busy with something." Aunt Katie pecked Roxie's cheek and went on her way too.

"I will. See you later," Roxie replied, but the other woman was already gone.

Roxie looked down at herself, still dressed in a white cotton nightgown and a robe. Getting a shower and putting some clothes on might be a good way to start the day, she decided. As she showered, she thought about calling a friend to meet for lunch, but which one? The only friends she had who knew about Lily were Nick and Wendy. Neither one had asked too many questions about why she'd never spoken about Lily before, but the others might.

Emily would probably be hurt that Roxie had never told her about the daughter who was hidden away, but she'd understand. Kitty and River, as well as Keily, would be understanding too, but Roxie hated the idea of going over and over the explanations one at a time. Which meant she should introduce them all to this new fact about herself at the same time. But a lunch full of people wasn't what she really wanted at the moment.

By the time she'd dried her hair and put on a pair of black leggings with a gray sweater that wasn't too heavy for the weather, she had talked herself out of lunch with anyone. Going back downstairs, her thoughts were on what to do instead, but the answer was there.

Lincoln was sitting at the kitchen table, dressed in his usual expensive suit, looking as if he'd just stepped out of a board meeting.

"Hello Roxie," he said without inflection or turning his head. "We need to talk."

"I suppose we do," she answered, going to the fridge to get some juice before she joined him at the table. "What do you want to talk about?"

"How things are going to go over the next couple of weeks," he told her as she sat down, his eyes on her at last.

She noted there was no emotion in his gaze and wondered if there was nothing left of that man she once thought might love her. That was a stupid thought, she decided and looked away from him. Looking into those emotionless eyes hurt too much.

For a brief moment yesterday, there'd been hope that he might come around, that he might see that she hadn't hidden Lily from him to hurt him. Then he'd caught her hugging Nick, and everything had turned dark again. So why was he here now? She knew what was going to happen over the next few weeks, he was going to be a dick and she'd do whatever it took to make sure she had some contact with her daughter once this was all over.

"What are you doing here, Lincoln?" She asked when the silence stretched out, when she couldn't stand it anymore. "We both know you're taking Lily from me, and we both know that we're done. What else is there to talk about?"

"I need you to sign the papers that will add me to her

birth certificate and sign over custody to me. I had my lawyer get everything together over the weekend and had it brought down to me this morning." He slid over the papers that were in front of him on the table, along with a pen. "That's all."

"Alright," Roxie murmured, her eyes on the papers. Her real name was on those papers, the birth name she'd avoided for so long now. She wasn't even sure if her signature would be the same now, since it had been years since she'd actually signed it. "Anything else?"

"No," Lincoln answered simply and sighed quietly.

Roxie took her time, looking over each piece of paper, signing the lines by the little stickers that said, 'sign here'. The papers for Lily's birth certificate were simple enough, but the papers signing over Lily's custody, already signed by Aunt Katie, nearly made her get up and walk away. There was no guarantee of visitation, no mention of how she could change things later, no hope that she would have any rights at all to her own daughter.

She looked up at Lincoln, her eyes dry because she'd already shed countless tears. "You're really going to take her away from me?"

"Yes, Roxie, I am." He didn't look at her, he looked out at the ocean and adjusted his tie. "She'll be safer. We've already agreed that."

"Yes, we did." Roxie put the pen down, a memory

suddenly coming back into her brain. "These guys you have tailing me, are they the same guys that June mentioned might have some kind of information I'd want?"

"I don't have any men tailing you, Roxie and what did June tell you?" A knot formed over the right side of his jaw, tension not allowing the knot to go away. He looked at her finally.

Guilt.

She saw guilt in his eyes.

But why?

"She said there were things you knew that you should have told me. That you had secrets of your own. I'd forgotten about it until now because of everything that's happened. What did she mean, Lincoln?" Roxie watched him, noting his expression.

"Your parents didn't kill themselves," he said after a long moment where she wondered if he'd get up and leave. "I know who killed them."

Roxie stared at him, unable to do anything but gape. "You knew they didn't kill themselves? Or that my father didn't kill my mother and then himself as the news people reported? You knew this and you didn't tell me? And holy fucking moly, you know who killed them?"

Roxie threw the papers at him and walked away from the table. "All this time you knew how I wanted to prove they were murdered, you knew how much this all hurt me, how it changed me, forced me to live in fear for my life, and Lily's, and you said fuck all to me?"

It didn't matter if she was screaming at him in his own house, or if he got angry and told her to leave, or better yet walked away, because whatever she might have hidden from him, she'd done out of fear for Lily. This? This was some whole next-level bullshit.

"I wanted to find the proof that would convict them, Roxie, before I told you," he started but she held a hand up, stopping the flow of words.

"You're no better than me, Lincoln. Only I'm not trying to hide your daughter from you anymore or take her from you. You knew a secret that could change my life, set me free, but you chose not to tell me. And on top of that, you want to take my daughter from me? No, no this is not happening."

She walked out of the kitchen, but he stopped her, grabbing her arm to turn her around. "I did it to keep you safe."

"You mean like I did to keep Lily safe, only you shattered my heart and then set it on fire with your demands for custody. Do you mean like that, Lincoln? Is it because you hate me or because I hate you? Because I can tell you this for nothing, I will never, ever forgive you for this. Any of it."

"Roxie," he started but she shook her head.

"No, I don't want to hear it. I don't know what I did in a past life to deserve the absolute fuck-me-over-fest my life has been, but I'm done with it. I'm done letting you treat me like shit because I tried to protect our daughter, and I'm done being treated like dirt by men. Just go, Lincoln. I don't want to look at you right now. And to think, I thought you were better than the other men I've known in my life." She looked at him, not bothering to hide her disgust, jerked her arm from his grip, and walked away.

"Roxie, please, let me explain," he called out, but all she could hear was her begging him to let her do the same thing.

Well, Lincoln Young was about to get the same exact treatment he'd given her. She didn't know how she was going to do it, or what exactly it was she was going to do, but she knew one thing - She would do whatever it took to pay him back for exactly what he'd done to her.

Roxie went out to the hall, grabbed her bag, and left the house. It was Lincoln's house. She didn't want to be there anymore. Let him have it. She'd pick Lily up from school when it was done and somehow they'd make do in her old apartment. Thankfully she hadn't signed any of the custody papers. Lincoln would have to take her to court for that.

Of course, this meant someone would have to pack up all their stuff and bring it over to her place, but she'd ask Aunt Katie if she'd mind doing that. Her phone started going off about the time she reached her apartment door and opened it.

"Fuck you, Lincoln," she muttered and turned the phone off for now. Later, she'd turn it back on and let Lily know there'd been a change in plans.

Who knew, Aunt Katie might decide it was better to take Lily back to New York after all of this. Roxie didn't really want that, especially now that Lily had been enrolled in school down here and had her heart set on meeting new people. Okay, on getting to know her father, Roxie had to admit to herself as she sat down on the couch Wendy had replaced when the old one was shredded by Nathan.

Fuck, this was one huge mess, and she had no idea how to fix any of it. Maybe for now, it was best to let Lily stay at Lincoln's until she could find a bigger place that she could afford. And then what? Go back to spending her nights dancing while her child slept at home with no mother there, only Aunt Katie? Could she really do that to Lily?

The tears that Roxie had thought were all dried up sprang back into her eyes as she remembered she'd promised Lily she would be at the house when she came home from school. None of this was fair to Lily, and it was all because her parents had made some very stupid decisions one night a long time ago, when very bad people had destroyed Roxie's life.

She couldn't make Lily pay for those mistakes, but she didn't want to lose her daughter either. So just what the fuck was she supposed to do now?

Lincoln

*L*incoln jumped when his phone buzzed in his hand. He'd been calling and texting Roxie, but there'd been no answer. He was worried about her and lost in the things she'd said to him, so the gentle buzz surprised him.

A frown formed between his eyes when he saw it was one of his security people stationed outside. He answered the call, not wanting to be bothered but they wouldn't call unless there was a reason. "What's up?"

"Um, Mr. Young, there's a woman here who says she's your mother. Shall I let her through?"

Oh, fucking hell, just what he needed. His mother here to berate him and tell him what a stupid boy he'd been. Fucking great.

"Let her in. It's fine." Lincoln hung up with a heavy sigh, his hands over his eyes. As if this mess wasn't bad enough, now his mother was here. That was the last thing he needed.

He heard a car pull up and walked to the door to open it.

"Hello, mother," he said simply as she stepped into the house, a yellow wide-brimmed hat that matched the tailored dress she wore smacking him in the face.

"Hello, Lincoln. I hear there's been some trouble," she said as she turned to face him while he closed the door. Her brown eyes were hidden by very dark sunglasses, but her lips were pursed in question.

"A little yes. Come in. Would you like something to drink?" He asked, and rolled up the sleeves of his shirt, the jacket and vest long-since discarded.

"Just coffee, please, son." Ms. Young walked into the house behind him, judging everything if he knew her at all.

Lincoln produced the coffee in silence, added every-thing to a tray, and took it to the kitchen table where she'd settled. He saw she was glancing over the papers that Roxie had left behind, the sunglasses gone, her hard eyes now on him. "What's all this?"

"Part of the trouble." Lincoln took his own cup of coffee and sat down at the table. There wasn't much use in lying to her, she'd figure it all out eventually anyway.

"Who is this Roxie woman June told me about," Ms. Young asked, pushing the papers away, obviously not worth her time so she dismissed them.

"Roxie is Chloe, mother. Chloe Abshire." Lincoln nodded at the papers but kept his eyes on his mother.

"Chloe Abshire, is she that girl you had a crush on in high school?" His mother tapped at her chin, lost in thought before she brought her eyes back to her son. "The one that disappeared?"

"No, I didn't have a crush on her in high school, but yes, she's the one that disappeared," Lincoln responded, trying not to get impatient. His mother had her ways, most of them annoying.

"Oh, I could tell you were in love with her, Lincoln. A mother knows." She smiled at him, that grin of knowing that infuriated him sometimes. At other times, it just left him amazed. "You didn't have a steady girl-friend all through school, and the girls were around you like flies with your pretty face and swimmer's body."

Lincoln felt himself flush as his mother talked about his body, something he wasn't exactly comfortable with. "I didn't have time for a girlfriend, mother."

"Protest all you like, but I saw how you watched June's little friend whenever she was at the house. Besides, I saw the notes. You adored that girl." Ms. Young waited for his denial, the smile still there, but her eyes watching him.

"What notes?" He asked, his skin blanched and he suddenly felt sweaty. She couldn't mean *those* notes?

"The notes she thought were from Liam, my love," she finally answered, and he felt his stomach plunge somewhere around his feet. That knowing look was back in place and Lincoln wanted to just disappear into a dark void. His mother had read his notes to Chloe?

Fucking hell, this was worse than he'd thought it would be.

"Why couldn't you have respected my privacy, mother? Why did you have to read those notes?" Anger was replacing embarrassment now and he didn't bother to hide it. "Normal mothers don't read their children's love letters."

'Oh we all do, son, don't be fooled. Besides, would you rather I didn't tell you I'd read them? Mothers always know what their children are up to, I've told you that before." She finally picked up her coffee, sipped at it, then put it down to look at Lincoln. "There's nothing abnormal about keeping an eye on your children."

"There is when it's about love and sex, and teenage…" He waved his hands, not wanting to say the words, but her silence forced him to. "Desires."

"That's nothing to be ashamed of, Lincoln. She was a lovely girl, and quite the handful now from what I hear from June." His mother's smile was back in place but there was nothing catty or knowing in this smile. It was just…a smile.

"Mother, seriously. Please don't. You've always been the coolest mother in the world, but this is none of your business and having you in my business now is kind of weird."

"Are you or are you not still my child?" She asked with a raised eyebrow. That eyebrow was a warning that he didn't heed. Still, she went on. "Your grandfather would have said I don't behave like a good Chinese woman should, but look where that's got most of them."

Lincoln didn't say anything, and finally, his mother took off her hat, slipped out of the black heels on her feet, and looked at him. "You're tired and aren't eating enough."

She got up and looked in cupboards until she found an apron and put it on. He knew it was useless to protest as she looked through the fridge and freezer to find the ingredients to make his favorite meal. "So, this woman had a child for you?"

"Yes, her name is Lily," Lincoln answered, turning to watch his mother chop vegetables.

"And you didn't know it?" Ms. Young continued to chop, but her eyes were on Lincoln.

"No, she hid the girl from me. Like you hid me from my father."

"That was for a very good reason, Lincoln," Ms. Young answered, pointing the knife at him.

"Who was my father, mother?" He asked, wondering if now would be the time when she would finally reveal the truth.

"You're old enough now, I suppose you can know the truth." She sighed as if she had the world on her shoulders before she shrugged. "His name was Colin Firth."

"Colin Firth? Colin Firth the actor?" Lincoln sputtered, then glared at his mother. "Stop messing with me, Mother."

"Fine." Ms. Young lifted her hands in the air and glared back at him. "His name was Colin Fuller."

"Colin Fuller. Okay." Lincoln had no idea who that might be, the name wasn't one in their circle. But then, it wouldn't be, would it?

"We had a lot of fun together at first. We were young, wild, experimenting with alcohol and other things I don't care to remember." Ms. Young shuddered and Lincoln knew not to push. "Then I realized I was pregnant. I stopped drinking because of you, but your father didn't."

Lincoln kept quiet, letting his mother work her way around the story he'd waited decades to hear.

"I wanted to be the best mother to you that I could be, even before you were born, so I tried to eat good food and not drink anything bad. Your father kept at it, and I came to realize being with him wasn't so fun anymore, but I had you to think of. I wanted more for you and to have a home, but we had no money, and everything became so stressful. Really stressful."

Ms. Young paused, her hands still as memories played across her face as emotions. "Your father got violent, especially when he was drunk. Very violent. Only, he'd forget the next day and ask me what happened to my face. Of course, he'd apologize, swear it would never happen again, then act like nothing had happened. Only it happened over and over again, until I finally ran one day."

She came back to reality for a moment, looking at him with so much love it nearly melted his heart.

"I couldn't let him hurt you the way he was hurting me. I knew he would if I stayed, so I ran away. I thought about giving you up once you were born, but I couldn't. I wasn't speaking to my parents at the time so I couldn't ask them for help, but I found a job at a Chinese restaurant. The owner let me live in the apartment upstairs, even though it was cramped. It was a two-bedroom apartment, one for men, one for women. There were already three other women in the girl's room, and two men in the other. I decided we couldn't stay in that situation and with the help of the restaurant owner's wife, I found a rich man to marry."

"That was the first man I thought was my father,"

Lincoln said, his memories of that man not very pleasant. Not terrible, just not pleasant.

"No, I thought things with him would be fine, even if I didn't love him. Then I found out that he really didn't like you. That changed things," Ms. Young said with a shrug of her shoulders, as if one man was as good as the next. "That's when I took up with his friend. He loved me, he accepted you, and it was alright for a little while."

"But you still weren't happy," Lincoln asked, some aspects of his childhood suddenly becoming clear.

"My love-life is a mess, Lincoln, it always will be. I didn't have your upbringing and I've done what I had to do in order to take care of my children. I've wanted the best for all of you, and I'm sorry if that made life hard for you, but you know? We're all human, we make mistakes. Huge ones sometimes, especially when it involves our children and their safety."

Lincoln suspected his mother knew everything about Roxie and Lily before she'd even arrived here, including how Lincoln had tossed Roxie out for not telling him about Lily.

"This Chloe woman, Roxie as she wants to be called now. She made choices when she was very young and very afraid, Lincoln. You're a man now, but even as a young man you wouldn't have understood the position she was in. I do, and I know why she made her choices. She made them for her daughter." Ms. Young glared at him, letting a smidgen of anger show through. Yep, she knew everything.

"I really messed up, didn't I?" Lincoln asked, not wanting to eat the food his mother now put in front of him, but she handed him a fork with a forceful look that brooked no argument. He began to eat while she sat across from him.

"You have, indeed. I wish you'd called me before you went and made a mess of all of this. I know I'm not the greatest with emotion, though I might be the coolest as you pointed out, but I'm not good at some things. I've had to hide a lot about who I was, what I am, to get where I am now. In order to survive, not to hide the truth from people. Men don't have it as hard as women in a lot of situations, and I know where this young woman was and is coming from because I've been in her shoes. You messed up, Lincoln. You need to fix it."

"But what if I end up like my father?" He asked, asking a question he didn't really want to ask but needed to have an answer to.

"Lincoln, you are nothing like him, I can assure you of that. You are good, gentle, kind. You are a hard busi-nessman, but when it comes to those you love, you have so much to give. You have an opportunity with this woman, a really good one, and a chance at true love. That's something I've never had from a man, and I want all my children to experience it. If there's a way to make this right with her, you have to. For both of your sakes. Don't end up like me, please?"

Lincoln finished the food and moved the bowl away to take her hands. "I think it might be too late already, mother. I've messed up even worse. I didn't tell her the secret I had been keeping from her."

"Oh?" His mother asked, truly surprised. "What's that?"

"I know who killed her parents," he said bluntly, wiping his mouth with a napkin before he sat back to look at her. "I just need a little more proof before I go to the police."

"Lincoln! How could you keep something like that from her?" His mother's anger was sudden and fierce, much as Roxie's had been. "I can't believe you did that."

"I didn't do it on purpose. One thing led to another, and the time was never right." Which were the exact words Roxie had said to him when she tried to explain why she hadn't told him about Lily.

Damn. He really had fucked this all up.

"That's always the way." Ms. Young nodded, understanding. "Still, you should have told her something."

"I know," Lincoln admitted, wondering how he'd make this right if Roxie wouldn't answer him.

Ms. Young took the bowl, washed the dishes, and put everything away while Lincoln pondered what to do next. He'd made up his mind to go find Roxie by the time his mother had finished.

"Well, your daughter will be home from school soon and I would like to meet her under better circumstances. I'll only be a phone call away."

"You don't want to meet her now?" Lincoln asked, confused.

"No, Lincoln. I want to meet her when her family is complete, and she can greet me knowing that I'll be the best grandmother a child could have. I don't want her to meet me when I'm another stranger who's a threat to the life she knows." She kissed the top of his head, patted his shoulder, and moved away. "You see? A mother always knows."

"I guess you do, thanks." Lincoln squeezed her right hand with love before she left the kitchen. He decided he'd wait for Lily to get home with Aunt Katie then he'd go find Roxie. His mother was right. It was time to make his family complete.

Without Roxie here, there wasn't much of a family, and he wanted only the best for his daughter. That included having her mother at his side, in the relationship he'd wanted since he'd first loved her as Chloe.

Lincoln

"Where's Mommy?" Lily asked as she came into the house, a smile on her face. "I want to tell her about my new friends. And my new teachers."

"She's not here, honey. She had to sort some things out, so I stayed here to wait for you." Lincoln lied, hating himself for it, but he couldn't really explain the argument with Roxie to a nine-year-old.

"Oh, I'll tell her later then. Do we have apple juice?" Lily went to the fridge while Katie came in with bags filling her hands.

"There's juice in the fridge, young lady. Hello, Mr. Young," Katie said, putting the bags down.

"Hello, Katie, and please, call me Lincoln as I've asked," he said kindly, noting how the woman's cheeks were flushed with exertion. "You should have told me you had all that, I'd have come to help you."

"Oh, it's just uniforms for Lily and some clothes for when she's not at school. I also got her some more school supplies and a few other things," Katie answered and went to check Lily hadn't made a mess with the juice. "I'll take them up and put them away."

"I'll help you, Aunt Katie," Lily said happily, and Lincoln smiled.

"Actually, I have an errand to run if you two are good for a little while?" Lincoln looked at his daughter and Katie, who both nodded.

"We'll be fine, Mr. er, I mean, Lincoln." Katie blushed, her pretty pale cheeks turning bright red. "I'll start dinner, shall I?"

"If you'd like. My mother was just here and fed me enough to feed all of us, so don't worry about me. I may be a little while, so don't wait up."

"Is everything alright, Lincoln?" Katie asked, her brows together in worry. Had it been something she said?

"Uh, Roxie and I had a bit of a spat earlier, I'm just going out to find her," Lincoln whispered so that Lily wouldn't hear.

"Ah, I understand. No worries, we'll entertain ourselves this evening." Katie nodded and shooed at Lily. "Grab a bag, girl, and let's get upstairs."

"See you later, Daddy," Lily called, and Lincoln couldn't help but smile.

"See you later, munchkin," Lincoln answered as he left the house.

Now, where would a very pissed-off woman who'd just been completely heartbroken go? Back to Nick's? He drove over to the building but didn't find Roxie's car there. He thought about the hotel she used to stay at, but she wasn't there either.

Next, he drove over to her apartment above Lemon Fresh, but her car wasn't there either. Lincoln drove away, thinking as he drove, going through the names in his contact list.

His first call was to Wendy.

"Hey, Lincoln, how are you?" Wendy asked, though it was obvious in her voice that she was confused why he was calling her.

"I'm fine, Wendy. I'm just trying to locate Roxie. You haven't seen her, have you?" He asked as nonchalantly as he could.

"Noooo," Wendy said, drawling out the word. "But now you have me worried."

"I'm sure it's nothing. I didn't mean to worry you, but

call me if you hear from her, alright?" Lincoln said, suddenly remembering how Roxie had said there'd been cars trailing her lately.

He'd dismissed it, assuming she was either being paranoid or the people had been with Nick. But what if she wasn't paranoid and they weren't Nick's people? Fuck.

He flicked through phone numbers until the one person he didn't want to call showed up on his screen. Nick.

Lincoln pulled into a parking lot and stared at the name.

She'd run to the guy when Lincoln kicked her out of his house, and said he was one of her best friends. Lincoln knew for a fact the man wanted much more than friendship from Roxie, but she didn't seem to notice that. Not even when he'd caught the guy kissing her. Even then, she'd acted like it had been nothing.

She was madder that he'd acted like a dick to Nick than she was about the guy kissing her. It was obvious that's who she'd run to now, so as much as he might hate it, Lincoln knew he'd have to call the asshole.

"Hello?" Nick asked when he picked up the call.

"Hi, Nick. It's Lincoln Young," he said, trying not to sneer into the phone.

"Lincoln. What can I do for you?" Nick asked, as

calm as he always was, even when Lincoln was antagonizing him. Prick.

"You can tell me where Roxie is," Lincoln said, leaving off the slurs he really wanted to use.

"Pardon?" Nick asked, obviously unperturbed by the barely-there veil of civility Lincoln was using.

"Roxie left the house earlier and she's not back yet. Is she with you?"

"No, Lincoln she's not. I haven't heard from her today."

"Right, like you'd tell me if she was standing right there in front of you," Lincoln said, wanting to knock the guy's teeth out.

"Look, Lincoln, it's no secret I don't think you deserve Roxie, but she sees something in you. I don't see it, but I'm not her." Nick laughed, a laugh that had a very definite 'fuck you' in it, but Lincoln let it go. "I'm at my apartment now, you can come here if you'd like, to prove I'm being honest."

"Fine, give me the address." Lincoln jotted it down and drove to Nick's place, knowing that he was probably going to make another mistake doing this, but he needed to know for sure that Roxie wasn't with Nick. If she wasn't, that might mean something much worse was going on. Something he didn't want to think about. At all.

Nick met him at the door to the penthouse, holding it wide open for Lincoln to see. "Have a look around, she's not here, man."

"Yeah, right," Lincoln said, storming through the place until he finally had to admit Roxie wasn't there. "Did she leave knowing I was on my way?"

"Not at all, as I said to you on the phone, I haven't heard from her today." Nick lounged against the wall, his face bland and unbothered. "You've obviously fucked up again, and if she hasn't contacted me, then she doesn't want to talk to anybody right now. The best thing to do is respect that."

"Listen, I've had about enough of you. She lets you run your mouth about me, but I can't do the same? Fuck you, Nick." Lincoln started to walk away, but Nick chuckled a sound that just…irked Lincoln too much to ignore.

"No, fuck you, Lincoln. As I said, you don't deserve her, and hopefully, she's had enough of your bullshit now and will let me give her the life she deserves."

Lincoln didn't exactly mean to do it, but he didn't do anything to stop the fist that was suddenly racing at Nick's right cheek either. Nick took the punch, landed a few of his own, but Lincoln had the upper hand. Nick was pinned to the ground, Lincoln sitting on top of him when Nick spit out blood against the wall with a laugh.

"You really think this will impress her? You really don't know anything about her, or the life she's lived all these years, do you?" Nick continued to laugh and pushed Lincoln away. "Let me tell you a little bit about the Roxie you think you know."

Nick went into the bathroom while Lincoln slouched against the wall. The fight was all out of him, and he had a feeling he deserved whatever Nick was about to tell him.

"I've known her for years now. She's always beautiful, always happy, and you'd think her life is perfect, that she's doing well. But on the inside? That girl has some serious baggage, baggage that you're a part of. Can you imagine being her? Her parents were killed, she winds up pregnant and alone, doesn't want to ruin your life, and is so afraid of whoever those men were that beat up her dad that she runs away, even from her child." Nick's voice was muffled as he ran water in the bathroom but became clearer when he came out with two wet washcloths and handed one to Lincoln. "She builds up a business for herself, maybe not the first career many women would think of, but she does alright, makes a name for herself, and keeps it together. She sends money to the kid she's got hidden away, goes to see her when she can, then in you walk, larger than life, offering her the world on a platter."

Nick went to a cabinet, poured out two measures of

scotch into two glasses, and handed one to Lincoln, now that he'd wiped the blood from his nose and mouth. "Now, she's got this guy, this know-it-all asshole who promises that he's going to be better than the last asshole who used to knock her around and steal from her. That actually put her life in danger, then yours of course, I haven't forgotten what Nathan did to you."

Nick stood in his own hallway, looking down at Lincoln, obviously enjoying taking Lincoln down a notch or two. "You give her the stars and the moon, until you disappear. Then you come back and she's, and I hate to say this because she didn't say it, I could just see it in her eyes, but the girl was hearing wedding bells."

Nick slid down the wall across from Lincoln, staring at him with a hate that Lincoln knew he deserved. "Then you throw her away."

"That's not what I meant to do."

"But it's exactly what you did. And I'm guessing whatever you did today was ten times worse if you have no idea where she is. So, what did you do this time, motherfucker?"

Lincoln wanted to punch Nick again for that last jab, but instead, he wiped his mouth with the washcloth, then his knuckles. "I told her the truth."

"And that is?" Nick asked, his eyebrows up in question.

"I know who was behind her parents' deaths,"

Lincoln answered, not sure why, but spilling his guts anyway.

"I see. Yeah. That's fucked up, Lincoln." Nick nodded, took another sip of his drink, then let it dangle between his knees. "I reckon you're just about fucked now."

"What do you mean?" Lincoln sat up, slugged the drink back, and put the glass down, ready to go.

"You kept that information from her. I don't see a way for you to come back from that after everything else you've done. Including taking her daughter from her, did I forget that part?" Nick looked up, as if thinking, then looked back down at Lincoln with obvious hate on his face. "Even if I knew where she was, I wouldn't tell you."

"Thanks for that, man." Lincoln got up, done with the game Nick was playing, and made to leave.

"I can tell you this much, Lincoln. You need to figure it out. If you loved Roxie, you'd know where she is. And you wouldn't be at my place, trying to beat the shit out of me." Nick laughed again, a laugh that continued to mock Lincoln as he left the place, closing the door behind him.

Nick was right, Lincoln was fucked.

He had no idea where Roxie could be. He had a list of people she knew, places she might be, but was she off somewhere licking the latest wounds he'd inflicted on her? Which made him think about what he'd asked his mother earlier. What if he was like his father?

Okay, he'd never laid a hand on Roxie in anger, but emotional wounds lasted just as long, didn't they? Because even though physical wounds might heal, the memories remained, and it was the same way with emotional scars. So yeah, he might not have hit her, but he'd hurt her, and he'd never forgive himself for that. Ever.

Lincoln drove home, hoping Aunt Katie or even Lily would have heard from her by now. Hours had passed, it was dark, and his phone still showed no contact from her. Before he went into the house, he called a number and waited for a voice to answer.

"Yes?" The voice asked and Lincoln spoke.

"Trace Roxie's phone. When you have her, tell me where she is." He hadn't wanted to do that, but now he was worried. Now he'd started to wonder if he'd wasted too much time already.

Lincoln walked into the house and found Lily asleep on the couch with Katie in a recliner not far away. He looked at her questioningly, but she shook her head. Fuck. He nodded toward the kitchen and Katie followed him in there.

"I'm worried. She should have contacted you or Lily. Have you checked Lily's phone since she's been asleep?" Lincoln whispered, getting enough ice from the freezer to fill a bowl. He stuck his hand in it and sat down at the table.

"I have, and no she hasn't contacted Lily either. Not since she fell asleep anyway. What is going on?"

Lincoln winced as the ice stung his skinned knuckles but relaxed when it began to soothe the ache away. "I've fucked up, excuse my language."

"No problem. What do we do?" Katie asked, staring at the bowl and Lincoln's hand in it.

"I call my people. We start searching for her. And if someone has her, they better hope I don't find them." Lincoln stood up with the bowl and headed up to his room. "I'll be back down in a bit. I have some calls to make."

Lincoln called Kai first, then Tanya to get her working on calling Roxie's friends. They'd all become friendly when Lincoln was missing, so that wasn't a problem. Kai was tracking her car and setting up a team to see if they could figure out Roxie's movements since she'd left Lincoln's house earlier that day.

Lincoln really wanted her to be holed up at Kitty's or drinking her cares away in some dive bar downtown, but his gut told him that wasn't going to be the situation. No, he'd been stupid, really fucking stupid over the last few days, and hadn't paid attention to the things Roxie had said to him. Now he suspected she was in real trouble, far worse trouble than he'd been in with

Nathan. Her life might actually be on the line, and he'd been too eaten up with jealousy and petty anger to hear what she'd said to him.

But please, he beamed out a desperate plea to the universe in general, if anyone is listening, please just let her be pissed off and drinking herself stupid and not where he suspected she was - In the clutches of a snake.

TWISTED INTENTION
~ A billionaire revenge romance series ~
Twisted Beauty
Twisted Love
Twisted Fate

Mafia's Obsession
~ A hot mafia romance series ~
Mafia's Dirty Secret
Mafia's Fake Bride
Mafia's Final Play

Screaming Demons
~ An MC romance series full of suspense ~
Rough Start
Rough Ride
Rough Choice
Rough Patch
Rough Return
Rough Road
Rough Trip
Rough Night
Rough Love

Standalone Contemporary Romance
Billionaire in Vegas
Billionaire Hunt

Billionaire's Game
Billionaire Retreat
Billionaire On Air
A Chance To Love
Somebody To Love
Not Mine To Love

Check out Summer's entire collection at
www.summercooper.com/books

ABOUT SUMMER COOPER

Thank you so much for reading. Without you, it wouldn't be possible for me to be a full-time author. I hope you enjoy reading my books as much as I do writing them.

Besides (obviously!) reading and writing, I also love cuddling my dogs, shouting at Alexa, being upside down (aka Yoga) and driving my family cray-cray!

Get in touch at
hello@summercooper.com
www.summercooper.com

facebook.com/summercooperauthor
instagram.com/summercooperauthor
goodreads.com/summercooper
bookbub.com/profile/summer-cooper